Shadows Over Seattle: Prequels 1-6

By Timothy Bateson

SHADOWS OVER SEATTLE: PREQUELS 1-6

First edition. April 30, 2024.

Copyright © 2024 Timothy Bateson.

ISBN: 979-8230682615

Written by Timothy Bateson.

Table of Contents

Dedication

So many people have been part of my writing journey and encouraged me to live this dream, and I'll never be able to thank them all personally. But the following people stand out above all others.

Joe Compton (of Go Indie Now) for providing his perspective on the first draft of "Wolves in the Desert." His experiences, insights, corrections, and feedback were invaluable in making the story what it is today. Without him, I know it wouldn't have the same level of authenticity.

The staff and owners of Fireside Books for their support of indie and local writers. They've hosted me for several book signings and events and have always been very supportive, easy to work with, and excellent hosts.

Anna Imagination (of The Healing Garden) helped me build my confidence as a writer and showed me what is possible when you make the right connections. I'd still be camera-shy if it weren't for Anna, Joe, and the entire Brain to Books Cycon experience. I'd also miss the interaction with readers and fellow authors and lack many of the organizational skills I learned from helping manage the Cycon events. I'm proud to count Anna as a friend and mentor and be part of her journey.

Elara Grace, for her amazing cover artwork. She took some of my initial ideas and put her own spin on them. Not only did she take my concepts into account, but she also asked for details about the character (Richard Parsons) and really brought him to life.

But, above all, I must thank my amazing wife, Sandi. Her first draft of "A Rose by Any Other Name" inspired me to write my own novel. She let me share the setting, steal one of her characters, and provided the basic outline for "The Challenge". My first novel is still in the works, but the backstories it inspired are contained in these pages.

Sandi has been my inspiration, biggest supporter, and the constant voice in my ear, driving me to finish the stories I've started and get them out to readers. As of writing these dedications, we've been married 19 wonderful years, and her feedback on my ideas has helped me expand her story into the Shadows Over Seattle setting, the short stories contained in these pages, and three planned novels (which will include an updated version of her original work).

Under A Hunter's Moon (Prequels #1)

Chapter One

October 31st, 2020

A janitorial closet was as good a hiding place as any while I waited for the museum staff to finish locking it up for the night. I'd allowed the door to lock behind me because that's how I'd found it when I picked it as my hiding spot. I also knew the night guard would probably check every door on her rounds.

I'd chosen this closet as a hiding place because it had a simple lock, which was important when opening it in the dark. I held my lock-picking tools while waiting and kept as quiet as possible. Thankfully, the overturned bucket I was sitting on wasn't too uncomfortable. I had to wait about half an hour before I heard the handle rattle and her footsteps retreat.

A couple of seconds working the lock was all I needed before I heard it disengage. I opened the door slowly, looking both ways down the corridor to ensure I wasn't spotted, before returning everything to where I'd found it. Closing the door again, I approached the main display area.

I had expected the display areas to be accessible, even at night, and was dismayed that the guard had closed and locked the heavy oak doors. This wasn't part of my plan and would slow me down from reaching my objective. The lock was more complicated than the one on the closet door, which was to be expected, considering the value of the display pieces on the other side.

I carefully ran my thumb over my lock-picking tools, selecting those I needed, and set to work. I glanced over my shoulder several times, thinking I heard movement from around the corner. I had no idea where the night guard was on her rounds, and I wanted to avoid bumping into her. It would ruin my plans if she discovered me so close to reaching my target.

Less than a minute after starting, the tumblers clicked into place. I opened the door and slipped into the room housing the touring exhibition. The green light from the emergency exit sign cast a pale glow over my shoulder. I shouldered my backpack and placed a folded piece of paper between the deadbolt and the strike plate, preventing the lock from engaging. I pulled on the door, which needed more than a casual effort to open—just how I wanted it.

The door opened into the rear of a large exhibition room, with dim overhead lights shining down on the displays. Moonlight drifted through the honey-combed skylight, causing filaments of shadow on the displays, like dark cobwebs. The clouds were so wispy that there was little chance of them blocking out the moon, which was good because having to switch on more lights would give away my presence.

The displays highlighted various predators and prey of Washington state. Different lighting effects created a feel of the wilderness and unsettled the nerves of the average visitor. But years of hunting at night meant that such tricks didn't affect me.

I glanced around, getting my bearings, and took in the life-and-death struggles that surrounded me. To the left, a rabbit ran from a cougar. Pheasants flew from bushes to the right, pursued by a raging boar.

Despite the familiarity of the other scenes, the central display caught my attention. The woodland recreation was so realistic that I even detected the scent of dampness in the soil. Two hunters hid in the bushes, pointing their rifles at a third figure. Though she wasn't human, I was familiar with her dual human and wolf natures.

She'd been posed in wolf form as if running from the hunters. As I reached out to touch her paw, I thought back to a night like the one depicted. My fingers touched perfectly preserved fur, and everything flooded back from that Halloween night.

The air turned damp, and the scent of the forest after rainfall filled my nostrils. Even though I was wearing boots, I felt the sensations of grass and mud between my toes. Tears welled up, blurring my vision, and as I looked up through the skylight, the moon became fuller and brighter—a blue moon that shone through the trees. The room faded.

Chapter Two

October 31st, 2001

The wolf lay panting for a moment before rising unsteadily. An old injury often made her transformations painful, and on this occasion, it left her breathless for a few moments.

I gave her time to gather herself, trying to ignore the scent of alcohol that wafted up with her every breath. Thanks to the lupine heritage I shared with this woman, my ability to distinguish odors was sharper than that of the average human. It made it easy to pick out the aroma of her favorite whiskey.

I glanced over my shoulder, ensuring the casual observer wouldn't spot our clothing. I fought back a stab of shame at their poor condition. Shape-shifters often wore loose clothing, but my mother had been buying from thrift stores ever since my father abandoned us. It would break her heart if she knew how much teasing I endured from the other gang members, but I loved her regardless.

My companion gave me a silent nod, and I started my shift into wolf form. I dropped to all fours and rose onto my fingers and toes. My joints and muscles rippled as my entire body changed in a process I'd never fully understood.

As my transformation finished, my perception of the world both narrowed and expanded at the same time. While my sense of smell had always been sharp, my wolf form could pick out a broader range of scents than my human form. The smell of the female beside me became as identifiable as her facial features and the red tints in her coat. My wolf eyes couldn't pick out the same range of colors as my human eyes would have. Reds had shifted into a muddy blur, yellows into creams, and blues were more vibrant. The reduced color depth didn't pose a problem because I was more attuned to the slightest movements around me.

I looked up between the overhead branches and saw the clouds were parting, revealing a clear disk of light. The moon shone down on the damp grass, causing it to glisten. We often went hunting under the full moon. It made seeing the prey a little easier, and I loved spending the time in wolf form. But tonight was also Halloween and a blue moon – the month's second full moon. There was no choice about changing to wolf form. The Hunter's Moon was the one time a lupine could not avoid his inner beast.

I stretched my limbs and pawed at the ground, reveling in the sensation. I had skipped dinner in anticipation of tonight's hunt, and my stomach tightened at the thought of biting into juicy prey. If we didn't catch anything, I would be hungry until breakfast, and my stomach growled at the thought.

My companion had several years on me, but she was as eager to hunt as I was. The speed at which she accelerated from a standing start to a run masked her injury. The maneuver was unexpected, and I found myself running in her wake. I had to increase my own pace to catch her. We both kept ourselves in good running form, but my youth was a definite advantage. I pulled alongside her flank in a few long paces, both of us on high alert for signs of movement or any other hint of prey.

Killing an animal the size of a small deer would leave too much meat. Instead, we planned on catching something smaller. Our target might be more elusive, but it would make a manageable meal. We ran for several miles before picking up the scent of suitable prey.

I caught a brief flash of movement to my right and watched the rabbit dart across the trail. I slowed down a little. My companion saw the hint and turned ahead as I turned on the rabbit's other side, so we flanked it. We worked our prey hard, snapping at its hindquarters. It tried to evade us several times, and we adjusted our tactics to accommodate. The chase ended as our prey ducked into a hole at the base of a burned-out tree stump, leaving us exhausted, chests heaving and still hungry.

CLICK-CLACK!

The sound of a pump-action rifle round being chambered brought my mind back to the clearing. My companion's head snapped around toward the source of the noise. I couldn't see the hunter, but I'd pinpointed his location. The sound gave away his position, although his scent remained hidden.

The wind shifted, and I realized he wasn't alone. I smelled at least two of them now. The scents of gun oil, leather, and sweat drifted toward me on the breeze. I tried to spot the second hunter, and my companion began moving forward as I did. One, two, three long strides toward the first hunter. She gathered herself to leap into the brush.

CRACK-BOOM!

The sound echoed through the trees as the second hunter fired. The shot came straight out of the bushes, its path untouched by the breeze.

Time slowed down.

I was already stepping away from the sound as the shot rang out. My mother's head snapped to the side as the bullet ripped through her neck before embedding itself in a tree.

I watched in horror as the impact drove my mother sideways. Spatters of blood missed me by inches, and my mother landed a few feet away from me. Somehow, she kept her feet under her, landing in a crouch. Blood dripped from her wound, but it didn't look as bad as I expected. For a moment, I thought that the bullet had clipped her rather than penetrated.

Locking her legs in challenge, she stood between me and the hunters. Her chest puffed up, and she started to growl, but the noise was barely a rattle. Blood dripped from her jaws as a look of pain and surprise crossed her face.

I can't imagine the force of will that kept my mother upright. But that willpower seemed to fade as she staggered once and then collapsed onto her side. Blood started to pool around her head and shoulders, soaking the ground and her fur.

Shock and horror held me in place momentarily, and then I stepped forward. I was running on instinct, not believing what I had just seen. Nor was I ready to accept my mother's death or that I would have to leave her. She lay so still, her chest barely moving, as her life drained away into the ground.

She must have sensed something because her eyes flashed open, and she focused behind me. It was the very last action my mother took. Her head dropped, her chest deflated one final time, and one last breath left her body.

I followed the direction of her gaze and spotted the barrel of a rifle poking through the bushes. A third hunter. This one had hidden upwind of us and had managed to stay undetected. Either my mother and I had stumbled into a well-executed trap, or the hunters were looking for other prey. Either way, the opportunity to bag themselves a wolf had presented itself, and they took it.

Insanity seemed to take control of my body, as the beast within bypassed any consent my brain might have given. My heart and mind turned icy calm as the raging beast prepared to give reign to its anger at my mother's death. The beast drove down all fear, common sense, or thought beyond its urge to kill. Beyond any doubt, I would die in the attempt.

I watched as my paw rose, and I took a step forward, followed by another. Like my mother before me, I was going to try to take down as many of these killers as possible before they killed me in return.

Even during my earliest transformations, I had never let the beast take complete control. It was like watching from outside my body. I accelerated into a sprint, and my muscles bunched up to power the leap, my speed fueling it. I felt numb to the guns, especially the one at my back. My mother's killer was going to feel the grip of my jaws at his throat as I tore my claws through his guts. He'd be dead long before his hidden colleague took his shot.

The moment before my paws left the ground, the third hunter took his shot. Stone shrapnel and earth struck my hindquarters as the ground to my left exploded.

The shock and pain were enough to thaw the ice in my veins. The world snapped into sharp focus, and I shook my head to clear the ringing in my ears. I needed to escape before the first hunter took a shot at me. I turned on the spot like a cornered beast, seeking escape from a cage.

A deer path looked to be the safest exit from the clearing. That meant having two guns pointed at my back. And that was a gauntlet that would normally terrify me. In its favor, that route put a tree between me and the one hunter who had not yet fired. I had no idea what lay in that direction, but I saw no alternatives. I poured my terror into my muscles and raced from the clearing as I tried to shake off the shock and out-race certain death. I dodged over uncertain ground and leaped over a fallen tree. The whistling of a near-miss reminded me why I was running.

I ran for a couple of miles before I started feeling guilty about leaving my mother behind like that. Although she was now dead, she had stuck beside me through everything.

Thinking about everything my mother had done for me, I resolved to give her a decent burial. I might not have been able to get revenge on her killers. But I would make sure they were unable to take the credit for a wolf kill or put her body on display in their homes.

As I decided, I realized I had been heading back toward the clearing where I had stashed our clothes. It was as if something in me reached out toward the familiar and safe. I could have tried howling for help from the pack, but I didn't know if anyone would have been in range to answer such a call. I would recover my mother's body tonight - alone.

The odds of being able to do so would decrease over time, so I had to think fast.

There was one place where I thought I could pick up the hunter's trail. I steeled myself for the potential horrors that I might have to face. Setting a cautious pace, I tried to keep all my senses tuned to my surroundings. A single surprise was all it had taken to put me in this position.

When I reached the clearing, the hunters had left, but their scents were still fresh. Scattered around the kill site were signs that they had moved the body hastily. Some scraps of rope and tarpaulin suggested they may have wrapped the body for transport.

This was good news in terms of being able to track the killers. The lack of body parts also showed that there had been insufficient time to gut the carcass. They would be carrying it whole. My mother weighed about a hundred and forty pounds, which would slow them.

As I sniffed around, I found traces of my mother's blood on the one remaining path out of the clearing. My nose told me that the hunters had all traveled together. They were heading back toward a wider trail used by campers to carry backpacks and hunting supplies deeper into the woods.

I followed them while keeping my distance. The hunters were not able to travel fast because they were carrying my mother's corpse between them, and I soon caught sight of them. As I suspected, they had wrapped it in a blue tarp and secured it with rope. Two of them carried the body, while the weapons and ammunition weighed down the third.

I thought about attacking the hunter with the weapons several times, but the risk was too great. He had all the guns, but only one needed to be ready to fire.

So, instead, I followed them back to their truck. As they were loading up, I kept to the shadows and tried to memorize their faces, the make and model of the vehicle, and the license plate. My mother's body was tied to the bed of the truck with bungee cords, and the guns were locked into boxes above the wheel wells. The three hunters climbed into the truck's cab and started the engine. I watched as one took a last look at their load and nodded to the driver before they headed back toward the main roads.

The drive was slow at first because of the roughness of the path, and I found it easy to trail them at a reasonable distance. None showed signs of seeing me in the rearview, but I kept off the path wherever possible. I crossed the path only to get better cover as they rounded a bend, and the gravel gave way to broken tarmac.

After another couple of miles, they turned onto a road that skirted the edge of the woodlands. The truck turned right, gunned the engine, and accelerated out of the junction. A moment later, another vehicle drove up behind them and sounded its siren. I watched as they pulled over and noticed one of the taillights was out.

The two police officers climbed out of their car, hands resting on their sidearms. The taller one stalked toward the driver's side while his colleague approached the vehicle's rear. As the first officer spoke to the driver, the brake lights and indicators flashed several times. A quick nod from his fellow officer confirmed that the taillight wasn't just cracked; it wasn't even functioning.

From my vantage point, the conversation at the front of the truck sounded friendly enough. The driver looked to be cooperating with the officer.

The second officer raised the tarp covering the guns and my mother's corpse, and everything changed. I heard the driver's tone get very defensive, and the first officer took a rapid step backward, moving the driver's documents to his left hand. His other hand rested on his pistol, thumb poised to snap the safety off.

As I watched, the second officer stepped away from the truck and returned to the patrol vehicle. He reached for the radio while focusing on the offending vehicle and his partner.

I lay down and forced myself to watch the scene unfold as the hunters were ordered out of the vehicle and onto the roadside. When a second patrol car arrived, everything from the truck's bed was loaded into its trunk, and the hunters divided between the two vehicles. I suspected that my mother's body would end up being used as evidence and then be destroyed.

I watched helplessly as the two patrol vehicles pulled away from the truck, leaving it at the roadside. Since there was little chance of following them, I closed my eyes and lay there shaking and gave in to the grief and despair.

I settled back on my haunches and let the beast speak for me. My howl split the air, calling into the night. The pain and rage in my voice echoed back to me from a multitude of sources, carrying many miles before dying away. A few voices joined mine as other pack members answered my call. In my heart, I could have sworn that my mother had joined them.

The tears flowed as I curled in upon myself, shifting back from wolf to human. The blurry darkness was comforting as I lay there, hugging my knees to my chest and rocking myself.

I don't know how much time passed before the familiar sound of paws approached through the undergrowth. I knew that I had to pull myself together. Rolling myself into a sitting position, I started to uncurl, my limbs protesting from having been held in one position for so long. As I sat up, trying to persuade my fingers to loosen their grip, I felt a gentle pressure falling on my shoulder.

I wiped away my tears with one hand and looked upward. My other hand reached out to remove the tightening grip, even if I had to break the owner's fingers.

My fingers met a huge hand roughened by the scarring left by years of hard work. Maybe the hand's owner sensed my intentions because the grip tightened as he crouched and looked me in the eyes. I could see his pain buried behind the concern. I'd lost a mother, and he had lost a pack member.

The bright full moon threw the man's face into sharp relief as I looked up.

Chapter Three

October 31st, 2020

The room snapped back into focus as I blinked and turned away from the spotlight that framed Art's features. He removed his hand from my shoulder, letting me rise under my own power.

"Richard, do you know why I told you about this exhibition?" I could hear the accusation in his voice.

"How did you find me?" I asked as I brushed at the dust on my knees.

Art smiled. "The same way that I found out your mother's remains were coming back here. The night guard is related to a pack member. Even though she's not one of us, you'd do well to keep in her good books. She was the one who recognized your mother's wolf form and called me."

"I know you didn't intend this to happen, but I won't risk losing her again. Do you know what happens to the exhibition once its run is finished? It gets broken down and hidden away again until the next time a wolf scares someone. Then they unpack it to remind people why these things happen."

"The cities are taking hunting ground from the wolf and lupine populations. That's the lesson displays like this are intended to teach, but that's not what happened to your mother."

Art steered me toward the display railing, and he leaned against it, his gaze on what remained of my mother. His big hands pointed at the expanse of the scene, and he was silent for a moment.

"Your mother never told you about the rogue lupine hunting the public trails, did she?"

I shook my head. My mother hadn't told me many things, including why she decided to hunt in that area when it wasn't our usual territory. Looking back on it, I hadn't even considered the lack of territorial challenge our presence should have warranted. It had been a full moon, so every lupine in the city would have been in wolf form, and almost all of us hunted in the woods and hills to the east.

"We couldn't have a lupine drawing attention to the rest of us. Police reports showed something unusual about the wolf and the killings. That's how it got my attention."

"Because we never interfere in the affairs of the wolves?"

"Except this time, there was a public outcry and demands for the city or state to announce a cull on the wolf population."

I nodded, seeing where this was going. "So, the pack stepped in and removed the rogue to prevent the cull from being approved." I followed the logic further: "They never voted on the cull, so my mother thought it safe to go hunting?"

"Except I suspect your mother went out looking for those hunters. I got wind that several hunters had been discussing finding the killer wolf and claiming it as a trophy." Art turned to me and looked me square in the eye. "I think your mother knew this and was looking to end her pain."

"Is that why she stank of alcohol? I suspected she'd been drinking again, but she seemed sober enough."

"She was never the same after your father left. I should have taken you to the police after she died. They'd have contacted your family looking for someone to take you in. But I couldn't bring myself to leave you there with all those memories, especially since your dad was the only person they might have reached. And I think we both know he'd have refused, and you'd have been sent into care." He paused for a moment. "Did you know your mother cried herself to sleep?"

I looked at him, the revelation bringing back a vivid memory. "She was crying over an old photo of her, me and my father, together. She asked me to stay home while she went and hunted, but I didn't want to be caged. I'd been at home too many nights and wanted to run."

"You can't blame yourself for what happened, Richard. No lupine likes being confined, but you were 12 years old and too eager to spend all your time in wolf form."

I leaned out and stroked my mother's fur and knew that despite the depression and drinking, she had loved me. She'd given her life, so I had a chance to live. Even though she had gone out there to end her own life, she had managed to see past it. In the end, she had defended the one thing in her life that still held importance... Me.

I put my hand on Art's arm, showing I was ready. He stopped momentarily as if saying his goodbyes to my mother. Then he picked up my backpack and handed it to me.

"Time to get back to the present. Isabella will let us out the side door. No one need be any the wiser. But beware, Richard, I won't always be able to bail you out of trouble."

The Lupine's Call (Prequels #2)

Chapter One

July 12th, 2021

As I closed the door to our apartment and turned left into the kitchen, my girlfriend came storming into the room. Taking one look at her, I knew I was in trouble, and I had a feeling that I knew why. Nazurl was usually even-tempered, but when I'd done something to upset her, she'd let me know with a look that could melt steel.

The look she wore now was one I'd never seen before and never wanted to see again. Her deep brown eyes flashed angrily, and I saw the storm brewing. She'd gone from being my Princess to a full-blown African Goddess of War.

I didn't even get a warning shot or a chance to compose myself before she launched her first offensive strike.

"Richard Evan Parsons..." Oh God, I was in real trouble. "I've been waiting over three hours for you to get home..." That meant she'd had time to build up a head of steam over whatever it was... Great.

I tried to interrupt by moving in for a hug, arms wide open, but was stopped by the sight of what she had in her hand. The amber liquid slopped around the inside of the bottle as she swung it in my direction, holding the neck and brandishing it like a club.

Seeing the liquid sloshing against the glass stopped me instantly; I was more worried about the whiskey than Nazurl's anger. One wrong move or word, and that precious liquid would be gone.

"Do you know where I found this?" Of course, I did, but I wisely decided not to answer the question. It was apparent where she'd found it and how. But I wasn't going to interrupt her because I was afraid I might say something I'd regret.

"I was getting out of the shower after my workout and found THIS behind the towels." That was precisely where I'd left it after opening it and draining half the bottle over a couple of hours.

Today would have been my mother's birthday, and I'd been trying to drown the memory in the bottom of a bottle. As soon as I realized I was halfway through the bottle, I'd hidden it quickly before heading to the store. I'd planned to grab another bottle but had forgotten to pick up my wallet. Instead, I was forced to grab a sandwich and use up the last of my loose change. I'd then walked downtown to try to sober up before Nazurl came home. Unfortunately, I'd lost track of time, and she'd beaten me home.

A loud thumping noise brought me back to the present as Nazurl slammed the bottle against the countertop. The liquid sloshing rang in my ears more than the sound of glass on granite. I tried to scan the bottle for cracks, but I didn't even get a chance to see the liquid settle before Nazurl slapped me and made me drop the sandwich.

If I'd thought my head was ringing before, it was nothing compared to how it felt after that blow.

I tried to pull my thoughts back together, but instead, I fumbled my words as I tried to come up with anything to stall her rising temper.

"I... I... I didn't even th... think I st... still had any bottles. We dumped the last of them last... weeks ago."

Her glare clearly showed that Nazurl didn't believe a word I said, and I didn't blame her.

We'd been together for almost three years and had argued about many things. In the early days, it had been small things, like what movies to watch, where to have dinner, or whose turn it was to pay. But then we moved into an apartment and shared it for about two years. The routine quickly changed from friendly disagreements to heated words and slammed doors. Mostly, it had been because Nazurl learned how bad my drinking habit was, but also because she was determined to break me of it.

Three months ago, that had culminated in me promising to get help, go to meetings, and dispose of four bottles of whiskey down the toilet.

I tried the meetings; I did. But there were too many people there who reminded me of what I'd become, and I'd given up going. Shortly after that, I was back to drinking and trying to hide it.

I'd gone out every night when I was supposed to be at meetings and just walked. Sometimes, I'd pick up a couple of shot bottles to tide me over until I could sneak a real drink. Getting home, I'd tell Nazurl some tale about the meeting, but I hated lying to her, and my temper had gone downhill fast.

I'd been lying to her since the day we met. Truthfully, it was a case of hiding something from her for her own safety and mine. The longer I hid the fact that I was a lupine, the harder it got to tell her.

Then, one day, she found hair on my clothing that didn't match her hair color or mine. How could I tell her that it was from my wolf form?

And that's when I started sneaking bottles back into the apartment.

That thought made me want a drink more than ever, and I made another in a series of mistakes. I stepped in as if to hug Nazurl, but my right hand betrayed my desire, and I reached for the bottle.

As my fingers caressed the smooth neck, Nazurl shoved it further back, beyond my reach.

"If you want this bottle, you're going to have to get through me," she said firmly.

I pressed against her, and her firm body resisted me as I stretched. I was almost close enough to kiss her lips when I felt her turn away. The moment it took for me to register the move was enough time for her to slam her hand into my chest, knocking the air from my lungs and driving me back a couple of paces.

It took several seconds for me to recover and get my breathing back under control; Nazurl didn't move a muscle or even blink. I'd always admired the control she had of her body and even enjoyed it. But now I had a new appreciation for what that meant. Except for her breathing, she may as well have been a statue.

Sidestepping, I tried to rescue the bottle, and a storm crossed her features.

Once again, Nazurl moved as fast as lightning, and I backed away. The rib-crushing blow that I was expecting never materialized. Instead, I heard breaking glass as the bottle smashed against the rim of the steel sink.

The metallic ring was nothing compared to the sound of precious whiskey gurgling down the drain. I didn't even get to mourn the last of my precious whiskey because Nazurl thrust the broken bottle between us. Light bounced off the razor-sharp edges, and again, Nazurl stood motionless. Even in her anger, Nazurl looked stunning, but I found it hard to drag my eyes away from the immediate threat of receiving a faceful of glass if I tried anything.

Then I watched as her expression turned to frost. She nodded once, acknowledging the standoff. Two or three seconds passed before either of us made a move, and as I blinked, Nazurl made the move that drove a massive wedge between us.

Turning at the hip, Nazurl brought her improvised weapon inches closer to me as she reached for the tap. Turning it on, she washed the last whiskey dregs down the drain, and I lost all hope of recovering anything from the situation.

"Fine. Have it your way." I growled in frustration and gave Nazurl one last look before making the third stupidest mistake of my life. Turning on my heel, I ignored the threat at my back as I stormed out of the apartment. I knew I was probably about to lose the love of my life, but I wasn't thinking straight.

As I left, I slammed the door behind me with enough force to rattle the frame. With another growl, I kept walking before I changed my mind and begged to be taken back.

Chapter Two

July 12th, 2021

It wasn't until I reached street level that I worried that I hadn't picked up my wallet and had left my cards upstairs. I was also out of cash to pick up another sandwich.

I shoved my hands into my pockets and felt the smooth leather of my wallet and cell phone case. To my relief, I wouldn't have to embarrass myself further by having to return home for anything.

There was a stiff breeze, and I caught the scent of impending rain as I headed toward the bank on the corner of 15th Avenue. A slight change in the air hinted at the coming weather change, but I had the experience of living on the streets and hunting in the wilderness. Being able to tell when weather changes are coming can make the difference between life and death or coming home smelling of a wet dog.

I hit up the ATM and drew out the last of my meager savings, not knowing how long it would be before I could face myself or Nazurl again. The money went into the same pocket as my cell phone, which I pulled out and turned off on a whim. I didn't want its annoyingly cheerful ringtone to upset my self-pity. Now I just had to decide where to go.

It didn't take me long to decide. There were very few people I considered friends, and most of them would be at work. I could have dropped in on Jimmy, but even though I was a well-known face at his office, he had an appointment. That was why I'd spent the day alone rather than with the only person who knew all my secrets.

We'd grown up on the streets together, and after the death of my mother, he'd become like a brother to me. The two of us had looked out for each other, and he tried to keep me out of trouble while I stood up to anyone who wanted to pull him into the gangs. Jimmy kept his nose clean and found a respectable job when we were old enough. Turning up at his office in my current state could easily blow the deal he was working on, and I couldn't do that to him.

I'd gone the other way, slipping into petty crime and retaining criminal ties even after we got out of school. But there was always a wild side that I had to hold back around the other kids. But Jimmy knew about it and what I was capable of.

That side of me begged to be let loose now, and I seriously considered taking a cab out toward Cougar Mountain. Hunting in wolf form gave me a chance to reflect on what was going on in my life and look at things more objectively. But I denied my inner wolf that chance. I was in too much of an emotional mess to subject that part of me to the turmoil.

Instead, I hailed a cab, and as I settled into the back seat, I gave the driver instructions to head for U-District, where I'd find my only other haven from the world.

While settling in for the ride, my mind kept going over the argument with Nazurl, and I was getting angrier by the minute. Thankfully, the cab ride was short and left me on University Way within a hundred yards of my destination.

I tipped the driver well because he'd put up with my mumbling and growling without a word, which I was thankful for. Had he said anything, I might have given him a piece of my mind, and he didn't deserve that. After all, he wasn't the cause of my mood.

I gave the driver time to pull back into traffic before ducking into the warren of alleyways between the stores and businesses. My destination lay about halfway down an alleyway between the two streets; most people didn't even know it existed. A powerful spell masked the Devil's Own from mortal eyes. If it hadn't, there was little about the exterior to draw attention. That was unless you noticed the lack of graffiti on the walls and the small plain sign that told you the doorway led to anything except the back of a business.

As I walked into the Devil's Own, a couple of heads turned in my direction but then looked away. The Devil's Own is a carefully guarded secret among members of the supernatural community, and most of us tend to stay out of each other's business. That fact alone made it one of the few places supernaturals could go without interference from mortals or local police.

It was quiet tonight, and I was grateful for that as I slipped into a booth in the back. I glared at anyone who looked my way as I flagged down one of the bar staff.

From where I sat, I could see the entire room except for the booths. But I already knew they were unoccupied, and I'd be able to see any new arrivals before they sat down.

Old habits die hard, and when the barmaid arrived, I ordered my usual social drink - a beer. It wouldn't mix well with the whisky already in my system, and I'd wake up with one hell of a hangover. But I wasn't thinking that far ahead. I needed a drink, and I needed it now.

As I settled in for the night, my thoughts kept turning back the clock and the angry words from earlier. It struck me as odd how quiet I'd been, given the level of anxiety and anger that had been bubbling on the surface. Maybe deep down, I'd known that I couldn't defend my actions. Or perhaps I'd been so engrossed in recovering the bottle that I couldn't form a coherent thought.

Bottle after bottle built up in front of me, and I refused to let the bar staff remove them as my thoughts kept churning over and over. I'd fallen back on old habits without a second thought, and I'd just walked out on the only woman who cared for me more than my mother had.

And that was the problem. I kept coming back to those thoughts. I'd lost my mother to hunters, and now I was losing Nazurl to my stupidity. I couldn't decide which was worse, and the drinks weren't helping.

A familiar voice pulled me out of my self-pity, and I ducked back further into the booth, hiding.

Only one person, besides Jimmy, had been there most of my life. And the Devil's Own was his bar. Thankfully, Art was a creature of habits too, though his were healthier than mine. I estimated it would take him a few minutes to circulate amongst his other customers before reaching my booth. That gave me time to slip out unnoticed.

I reached into my pocket to grab some cash for the tab when a large hand pushed me back into my seat. I hit the chair hard and looked down at the length of a massive arm.

Art wasn't happy. Standing at close to six feet in height and weighing over 250 pounds of muscle, he was an imposing figure. But I was used to seeing kindness in those green eyes that put people at ease. That mixture of hard and soft had made Art one of the most respected lupines in the city. While pack alpha was purely a human concept, it was one that the lupines had adopted, and it was easy to imagine how Art had risen to the position. Of course, there were plenty of rumors, but I knew he hadn't wanted the job and only challenged the old alpha out of necessity.

A scraping noise and a heavy sigh brought me back to the present again. Flicking some stray hair out of his face, Art settled into a seat opposite me, his back to the room. I never understood how people could leave themselves exposed like that. Maybe I had trust issues, but sometimes, I thought Art trusted too quickly. He wanted to see the best in people; he wasn't getting it from me. Hence his current mood.

Art's eyes dropped to the bottles on the table, and I watched that anger turn into an accusation and knew what was coming. We'd had this discussion before.

"Are you so ready to follow your mother into the grave? Because if you keep it up, that's exactly what will happen."

My anger grew. I wasn't putting up with this today of all days. A line was about to be crossed, and I wasn't sure which of us would push the button that detonated this conversation.

"Butt out, Art. You know what today is... Hell! You've gone to great lengths to make sure I keep my mother's memory alive. I have no intention of making the same mistakes."

The hand gripping my latest beer started shaking as my mind replayed the circumstances of her death. Nazurl hadn't remembered the date, and now I found myself judging the man who'd taken me under his wing after my mother's death.

"So what? You think Louise would be proud of what you're becoming?" Art asked as he moved the bottles out of the way. The look in his eyes reminded me of what I'd seen in Nazurl's and the one I sometimes saw in the mirror on those mornings when I questioned my life choices.

Art reached across the table and quickly plucked the drink from my hand. Sticking a finger in the neck of the bottle, he let it hang there for a moment before collecting three others in the same way.

"You're in no state to go home, and I'm not letting you do something stupid. When I found you out there in the woods, you told me your mother was dead, and I promised to take care of you. And that's what I'm going to do." With one hand full, he stood slowly, and the chair scraped back a little in the process. His look changed to determination, and he started to turn away, pushing the chair back under the table with his free hand.

"That's the last drink you're getting tonight. You can pay the tab another day. I'm calling you a cab right now. And then I'll call Nazurl and tell her to expect you so you don't stray." He had Nazurl's number? I'd never given him the number at our apartment or told him my girlfriend's name. Just how long had he been spying on me? The question must have shown on my face, or Art had become a mind-reader.

"Yeah, I know where you've been living. I know who you've been seeing. And you know I have my ways of finding things out. So sorry for caring about what happens to you."

My hands slammed down on the table, and I pushed myself to my feet before I realized that such a move could be read as a challenge to my pack alpha.

I tried to reign in my anger as I made to leave the booth but failed. I didn't care if I had to push past Art to escape, but he moved aside, making it easy on me. I got the sense he didn't want to fight any more than I did, but I'd hear about this incident later.

Unfortunately, sometimes later comes a lot sooner than you think.

As I passed him, Art grabbed the back of my shirt and hauled me off my feet one-handed. Considering my drunken state, I couldn't put up a fight against someone so much larger than me. With my feet dangling helplessly, I couldn't do anything except reach for his hand to try and pry it off my collar as he leaned in. I felt his warm breath against my ear as he whispered so softly that what he said was for my ears alone.

"I've told you before, Richard. Sober up, or things won't end well. You're a danger to yourself and those you claim to care about." He paused to let those words sink in. "Now, you're going to walk out those doors, climb in the cab that'll meet you on 15th, and go home to Nazurl and sober the hell up."

Setting me back on my feet, Art raised his voice just a little. Almost as if he intended others to hear his words.

"You're barred for the next week. After that, you come back, settle your tab, and we'll decide whether you'll be allowed back."

Dammit. By standing up to Art, I'd given him no choice but to reprimand me publicly. No matter how few people might have seen the confrontation, he'd lose face if he hadn't responded, and that would have hurt his standing as Alpha.

Art pointed to the door, but my stupid mouth opened itself again. I couldn't keep the venom out of my tone, even if I wanted to.

"I thought you, of all people, might have understood. You told me you mourned her death, too, but you seem to have gotten over it. I haven't. So, leave me to mourn her in my own way. You're not my father. That piece of shit decided to have nothing to do with me or my mother when I was young. So don't go preaching to me about how I should mark her birthday."

I spun on my heel, but not before catching a flash of something crossing Art's features. However, I'd pushed too hard, and Art was behind me the moment I turned, but thankfully, he just followed me as far as the door. That meant he was there to catch the vampire I shoved out of my way before slamming the door behind me.

Chapter Three

July 12th, 2021

I turned away from 15th Avenue, deliberately ignoring Art's instructions. The rain had started to fall while I'd been in the Devil's Own, and I had my head down to keep it out of my eyes. I'd forgotten how alcohol and anger can dull the senses and slow the wits. So, I wasn't aware of the figures following me down the alleyway that led to University Way.

When I raised my hand to hail a cab, I had my back to the alleyway. I was too focused on figuring out which vehicles were cabs as headlights bounced off the puddles on the sidewalks. That meant I didn't see the hands reaching to grab me until it was too late.

I was hauled back into the alleyway and thrown against the brick wall, shocking me back into sobriety and alertness. I didn't know how long this effect would last, so I had to take advantage of it swiftly. A quick look told me that I was facing two attackers. But a third entered my peripheral vision as I focused on the first two.

Both were tall and muscular, with features so perfectly matched in the darkness that they looked like twins. The new arrival stuck to the shadows and was probably the brains behind this group, while the twins were the thugs.

My assumption was proved right almost before I'd formulated it. The two grabbed me by the shoulders and lifted me off the ground, driving me up against the wall again. That was the moment that the third man stepped out of the shadows.

He was shorter and stocky, with a twinkle in his eye and a lop-sided smile. The glint of metal pulled my attention to the six-inch blade he drew from his boot. It was the second time today that I'd been threatened with a sharp object. But unlike with Nazurl, this blade wavered, giving away the wielder's nervousness or inexperience.

When he spoke, his tone told me he believed he had the upper hand, and I couldn't argue the point.

"Give us everything you have, and you might live through the night."

I was determined not to give them anything, even though I was outnumbered three to one. Thankfully, I was still angry at Art and myself, so I used that anger to fight back.

I pulled my legs up and kicked back against the wall hard, shoving the twins back a pace or two. They let go, and my weight was no longer supported by anything. I fell onto my knees, scraping my left a little.

Regardless of the injury, if I had any hope of getting out of this, I had to take advantage of their surprise.

I rolled away from the goons and into a crouch. The move left me room to throw myself at the leader's knife arm. I latched on with both hands because the sudden movement caused my head to spin. Fighting to focus, I shook my head and applied pressure against a nerve cluster and was rewarded with the clatter of metal against stone.

Finding the knife and kicking it away took me a precious moment. And that was long enough for the twins to have recovered from the shock of their victim fighting back.

It was still three against one, and I couldn't see a way to even the odds. These men smelled like mortals; I'd have an advantage if I shifted to wolf form. Just not enough of one to overcome three of them, especially since I'd have to strip before changing. Somehow, I didn't think I was going to get the chance.

But there was something even more profound that held me back from the change that my drunken mind insisted was the only way out of this. I was so used to hiding what I was from others that I didn't dare shift if there was a chance of leaving one alive as a witness. Humanity remained ignorant of supernaturals because we deliberately kept the number of witnesses low.

The change into wolf form would also take too long because the twins were closing in again. Given my condition, I was going to have to fight on their terms, and I wasn't comfortable with that. Even on my best days, I was a reasonable scrapper but not an accomplished fighter.

I threw several wild punches at the closest goon, landing a lucky blow to his windpipe as he tried to step inside my reach. He dropped hard, one hand going to his throat as he tried to suck in a lungful of air. Clone Two closed in with his hands outstretched for my own throat, and I dropped into a crouch, throwing a kick toward the leader, forcing him back a pace or two.

Clone Two's hands closed just above my head and caught in my hair, ripping out a chunk. I yelped and instinctively ducked even lower. That put my hands against the concrete, and I spun, kicking up and back.

Pain shot through my knee as my foot connected with something solid, and I heard a crunch of bone. Clone One winced in pain, and I saw him reaching for his ribs and wondered if I'd cracked or even broken something. I hoped that he had the sense to stay out of the fight, but somehow, I knew he'd fight harder, and I'd hurt for it later.

I tried to keep the twins in sight as I backed up toward the mouth of the alley. But it proved challenging to do and see what their leader was up to. That meant the knife swiping across my front came as something of a surprise, and I was lucky that it missed by a slim margin. My opponent was far from stupid and had used my distraction to try and take me out of the fight.

So far, I'd done okay, but I had no idea how to fight someone with a knife, and I was tiring quickly. The weapon gave him extended reach with a sharp edge. I was still stepping back in reaction to the first swipe when the second one came in with the knife in a reverse grip.

I couldn't tell you which of the twins grabbed my ankle, but I stumbled, and the blade cut through my shirt and scratched across my belly. I landed hard on my ass, with the wind knocked out of me before I could reflect on how bad that could have been. I barely avoided smashing my head open on the concrete by throwing my left hand behind me, shredding several layers of skin, and smacking my elbow against the wall.

I predicted the follow-up blow and threw up my right hand to try and fend off the knife, receiving a long gash along the forearm for my efforts. I pushed hard against the ground and used my attacker's proximity against him as I twisted my injured arm around and grabbed his wrist.

Using my opponent's arm for leverage, I pulled myself to my feet and kept moving forward, closing the distance between us. I twisted to bring the knife arm between us and used my body to pin his elbow against his stomach, taking the risk of getting a knife between the ribs. The forward momentum led to a headbutt, stunning us both long enough that he slipped on the wet ground and fell backward, pulling me down with him.

I thrust a knee up into his groin and rolled clear. Climbing to my feet, I stomped on his knife hand and kicked the blade clear.

I wasn't willing to trust my luck further and scrambled toward the street. I had to cross about a dozen yards, but my head was spinning, and it took me a few precious moments to get myself moving.

Once I managed to get my bearings, I continued stumbling for the street exit, but something was wrong with the lighting. I expected the streetlights to be muted from the rain, not strobing red and...

Dammit... Red and blue strobes. Police!

Facing potential charges of public intoxication and brawling, with enough wounds to prove both charges, I wasn't keen on running into a patrol. Because of my time with the gangs, I'd already spent more time in cells than I liked, and I wasn't about to add an extended stay to my list.

I had no illusions about what this incident would mean if I was captured. Even if the muggers were found and admitted their part in the altercation, there was a good chance that I'd still be tagged for aggravated assault. My rap sheet was too extensive for that one not to stick.

I doubled back, dodged around the muggers, and heard the shriek of brakes and running feet closing in from all sides. That could only mean that the police were combing the alleyways, too. I could have ducked back down the alleyway alongside The Devil's Own or into the bar, but I didn't want to risk running into Art again. He'd be very quick with an 'I told you so,' which was the last thing I needed.

I was nearly at the 15th Avenue exit when someone yelled for medical assistance and additional units. I kept running because the alleyways were too confined, and I'd be cornered quickly. Since the streets were open and more populated, there was less chance of the police opening fire on me if I could reach them.

As I burst out of the alleyway, several cruisers pulled up, doors opening even before they stopped. I heard a voice from behind yelling for me to stop, and I almost ran into a third officer as he got out of his car, already drawing his weapon.

I pushed on, diving into the oncoming traffic, and vaulted over the hood of a sedan to try and put something between me and the guns. I caught the driver's surprised expression, which would probably have been priceless under other circumstances.

Ducking between vehicles, I tried to hide the fact that I was heading toward 47th Street. I was now relying on my ears more than my eyes, and shouts were coming from all sides as the police coordinated.

A cruiser raced around the corner and pulled across the junction, blocking traffic and cutting off my only exit from the cordon. The net was closing, and the only way to 47th was to cut across the parking lot on the corner of the street, but it was a slim chance.

I was about to vault over the fence into the parking lot when I heard a screech of brakes and a meaty thump, which caused me to stumble as I tried to look back over my shoulder.

As I scrambled back to my feet, I heard someone yell, "Officer down," and decided that my freedom wasn't worth someone's life. I had to help, regardless of what it cost me.

I stepped out into the street and was about to raise my hands when I felt a sharp pain in my left shoulder. A second impact against the base of my spine had me looking over my shoulder just as a jolt ran through my entire nervous system.

My body stopped responding to commands, and I lost the ability to think. I dropped to one knee at first, but my body jolted over and over until my muscles gave up any pretense at keeping me upright. Thankfully, I was close to the sidewalk when my head hit the ground, and I lost consciousness.

Chapter Four

July 12th, 2021

When I came to, I was hurting all over, but thankfully, that pain reminded me that I was very much alive. Unfortunately, that also meant I was still very much alive, and that came with a whole pile of complications I wasn't ready to deal with.

It might have had something to do with the convulsions from the stun guns, but my head was throbbing. That was probably due to the drinks, so I employed my usual solution. I kept my eyes closed until I felt I could open them without the world spinning.

When I opened them, my vision was blurry but slowly cleared as I took stock of my physical condition. My head had fallen forward while I was unconscious, so I tipped it back upright, tasting blood in the process. I tried feeling around with my tongue in case I'd lost a tooth or cut my lip, but wherever I probed, I encountered pain.

It took a few moments to realize that the source of all the pain was, in fact, my tongue. I'd probably bitten it while getting the fight shocked out of me.

A glance confirmed that my wounds had been treated and dressed. It also led me to discover that I was seated in a metal chair. I'd been sitting in it for some time because it wasn't padded, yet it felt warm even through my clothing. In front of me, there was a steel desk of the kind used in some police interrogation rooms.

I tried to shuffle the seat backward so I had space to rise from the chair, but it didn't budge, and I felt a tightness around my ankles. A glance gave me all the explanation I needed. The chair and table were bolted to the steel plates of the floor, and my ankles had been shackled to the chair legs with thick leather restraints. My wrists had been similarly secured to the arms of the chair.

I looked around the room, and the steel theme continued. The walls were made from seamless steel plates held in place by steel pillars. A windowless door to my right continued the theme, making me think of bulkhead hatches on battleships. The first exception to the steel motif was a basic office chair tucked under the other side of the table, and the second was a large panel that looked like a mirror off to the left of the table.

I'd been in enough interview rooms to know that very few police stations could afford the two-way glass you see in the movies. So, it was unlikely that someone was watching me from the other side of the mirror, assessing my every move. But why would they install two-way glass when they already had cameras in the room?

The fact that I was being watched wasn't anything new, but the thought that someone considered me enough of a threat to put me in a steel box was.

No one was ever detained in a room like this, especially not by the regular police. There weren't the funds or resources to create a cell like this. So, whoever was holding me was unlikely to be Seattle's finest, which left me with no clue as to where I was being held, who by, or why the special accommodations.

I tried to get as comfortable in my seat as the restraints would allow. But steel is a particularly unyielding material, and now that I was awake, that firmness was becoming uncomfortable. My attempt to find a comfortable position had told me something else. My lockpicking tools weren't in my back pocket, where I usually kept them.

The odds were that I'd either dropped them in the street or someone had taken them off me as part of a routine body search. The former was unlikely because I'd stitched a liner into my back pocket to hold the leather roll. It was also my habit to button it closed when I pocketed my tools. So, that left the second possibility. Someone else had them, which meant that I had no way to get out of these restraints, even if my range of movement wasn't so restricted.

I suspected that my captors knew about my shapeshifting abilities, and if they did, they couldn't have picked a more thorough means to prevent me from shifting. The fact that I was still clothed presented the first of the risks because of the constricting effect of clothing on muscle groups that were rearranging themselves during the shifting process. I risked the possibility of tangling myself in the fabric and even choking myself to death, according to Art. I'd never taken the risk, in case he was right, but I still briefly considered the option until I realized that I might break more than a few bones as the restraints put pressure on my joints.

Maybe this was a military facility. They certainly had the kind of funding to build rooms like this. If that was the case, I had nothing to say except to ask for my phone call. Then, I just had to figure out who to call for help. So, I sat there for some time trying to decide if I should call Jimmy, Art, or Nazurl or try for a public defender instead.

It was sometime later, as I was beginning to wonder if my captors had forgotten about me, that something new happened.

A click came from the direction of the mirrored glass, and a section of the frame slid out a little way. When it stopped moving, a motor whirred into life, and a white projection screen unrolled in front of the mirror. Another click and whir came from above, and I didn't bother to look up, figuring it was probably a projector.

I was proved right when the lights dimmed a little, and an out-of-focus black-and-white picture appeared on the screen. As whoever was behind the projector made some adjustments, the image became sharper, and I realized that it was showing a grainy picture of me from just before the muggers attacked.

The angle wasn't ideal. It showed me starting to leave the alleyway and very little detail beyond that. There appeared to be something ghostly in the image, but I quickly guessed it was probably a reflection on a pane of glass in front of the camera. So, it was likely an image taken from a security camera in a store opposite the alleyway. The image rapidly changed several times, showing me being dragged into the alley and brief glimpses of the fight itself. I wished it had shown more because it wasn't clear from the angle what had happened.

The footage changed again, and now I was watching the police assembling for my capture. Some of the images came from angles that might have been dash cams. Others might have come from the eyes of the officers themselves. Of course, the latter was highly unlikely, so I guessed the local police had started using bodycams. That was new.

I watched myself run out of the alleyway, avoid the police officer getting out of the patrol car, and vault the sedan's hood. It was impossible not to notice that I wasn't entirely steady on my feet, despite any thoughts I might have had to the contrary at the time.

At that point, the playback stopped, flicking between frames as if it were being played from a VHS recording. Very few people still used VHS, so I tried to study the images to see if someone was trying to tell me something.

I still hadn't figured out the message, but a click from the doorway drew my attention back to the present.

Taking my eyes off the screen was hard. But, as the door opened, I had something new to focus on. A large shape stood in the doorway, blocking the entrance. I couldn't make out any details because they were backlit, almost as if someone had planned to intimidate me, but the room had already achieved that.

As he stepped forward, the expression on the man's face was enough to scare me all over again. He looked at me like dirt he'd scraped off the bottom of his shoe. And I looked back at him, all two-hundred-and-twenty pounds of toned muscle, trying to figure out his role in my captivity. The tight-fitting dark jeans, V-neck t-shirt, and short-cropped hair suggested that he might have been in the military at some point, even if he wasn't still active.

A quick look around the room seemed enough to confirm my visitor's expectations, and he pushed the door closed behind him. I expected to hear it click closed, but it didn't. I also expected him to sit opposite me, but that didn't happen either.

My head turned as far as possible while I followed his path into the room, but I lost sight of him when my neck wouldn't turn any further. Thankfully, that also meant I wasn't surprised when a heavy, scarred hand dropped onto my shoulder. The fact that he was close enough to breathe down my neck was a little disconcerting, especially given how warm that breath was.

"Where's your anger and rage now, wolf-boy?" came the harsh whisper in my ear, and the hand removed itself. He finished his circle around me, drawing my eyes back to the screen and away from the door.

I'd already guessed my captors might know about my abilities, but he'd just confirmed it. I was even more curious about who was behind all this because my guard was a follower of orders. There was something about his bearing and how he stood with his feet apart, back straight, hands behind his back.

The door clicked open again, and buzz-cut stiffened as if trying not to come to parade ground attention. I wasn't too keen on turning my eyes away from the man, but his full attention was on the door, so I turned mine there, too.

A rather large woman in her sixties stepped into the room as if she owned it, dominating the space by sheer presence and authority. Her blonde hair was streaked with grey, and the style added to her authority. She fiddled with something around her neck, and I spotted something like a bird skull on a chain. As the door closed behind her, I realized it was probably a crow skull or maybe a raven, and it was an actual skull, not a replica. There's something about the way light bounces off the bone that's a dead giveaway.

I thought I'd been curious before but now I was even more interested.

With a snap of her fingers, her pet soldier pulled the seat out on the opposite side of the table. She settled into it with a careless ease that showed her age hadn't resulted in any physical impairments. Another gesture and the picture on the screen switched to a police officer running into the road. It was probable that he'd come from the alleyway in pursuit of someone. Given the current context, I had little doubt that I was the one he'd been chasing.

"Officer Mortimer Talbot, Age 46, father of three, and days away from celebrating his twenty-fifth wedding anniversary. A twelve-year veteran of the Seattle PD, with awards for service to his community and city. Deceased."

The picture changed again, and we were now looking at the truck hitting Talbot. I winced as the woman continued speaking.

"Before we conduct any investigation into the incident, you're already looking at public intoxication, disorderly conduct, aggravated assault, and second-degree murder. Not bad for an evening's work".

She paused, probably to give the charges a chance to sink in.

"You're a wanted man, Mister Parsons, and Seattle PD isn't happy with you. Talbot was one of their own, so I can't promise that an accident wouldn't occur... if I were to return you to their custody... despite your special circumstances."

Whoever this woman was, she kept her composure and showed no signs of anxiety, nervousness, or any other hints that she might be lying or bluffing. She wasn't even sweating visibly. This woman didn't make idle threats, and she was probably the one who'd briefed the brute about my abilities.

She had my measure, and I'd seen enough movies to know where this conversation was going. So, I cut straight to the heart of things.

"This is where you offer me a deal I can't refuse, right?" I was frustrated that she had me at such a huge disadvantage. She wanted something from me and was willing to make a deal. However, I wasn't sure I'd be willing to pay whatever price she had in mind for what she hinted was on offer.

My restraints rattled slightly as I tried to lean forward and stare into her eyes. I'm not sure which of the two moves made the huge man growl, but I was sure he didn't appreciate the tone of my voice. That would be fine with me if he kept his distance.

The woman opposite smiled and shot a look at her colleague, who'd placed himself behind her right shoulder. Some unspoken understanding occurred between them, and he quieted. Then she turned back to me, and when she spoke, it seemed she was choosing her words carefully.

"Mister Parsons. For a price, I can pull a few strings and make certain aspects of the last few hours less..." She paused as if trying out the next part in her head, "...dangerous to your continued health and freedom."

I saw movement as her goon stepped forward, stopping right at her shoulder. His expression left no doubt as to what he thought of me, and he may even have been harboring ideas of jumping over the table and throttling me. But I also knew he wasn't the biggest threat in the room, so I pointedly ignored him.

"So, it's a simple choice I'm asking you to make. You may call it a bargain with the devil herself if it makes you feel any better about the outcome of the decision. But in any case, this will be better than any deal you'll get from a judge, based on the evidence against you, especially with your already extensive criminal record."

A trial wasn't in my favor, but I wasn't ready to concede to whatever she wanted. I was about to tell her as much when she jumped back in, cutting me off intentionally.

"You have three options. You can let this go to trial and hope the video evidence doesn't convince the jury of your guilt. But remember, you were resisting arrest, and a police officer was killed. That's not likely to earn you much empathy or sympathy. You could somehow break out of this room, escape my custody, and go on the run. If you do, you should change your last name to Kimble."

She gave me a brief smirk, which vanished almost as soon as I noticed it.

"Or you can hear me out and accept my deal." A key appeared in her hand, and she passed it to the brute. "Unlock his restraints, and if he gives you any trouble... Well, you know what to do."

As my shackles were unlocked, I made a point of fidgeting as little as possible, even though I longed to get up and stretch out muscles that felt like rubber after hours in the same position. The entire time, the woman watched me as she lounged back in the chair, perfectly at ease. When her cohort had finished unlocking me, he handed her the key and returned to his position, hovering at her shoulder.

"Firstly, you should know who you're dealing with and what power I have to make this offer." She smirked again as if enjoying the moment. "I'm Janice Cooperfield..." She paused as if letting the name sink in. I knew the name from somewhere but couldn't place it, so I kept listening.

"If you agree to my proposal, you'll call me Chief." A quick thumb over her shoulder pointed at the brute. "And you'll be saying yes-sir, no-sir, to Feldman here. He's one of my best operatives and would be your parole officer."

That raised a grin from Feldman that I didn't particularly like the look of. I guessed he had explicit instructions about what to do if I went back on whatever deal was about to be proposed. Assuming I agreed to the terms in the first place.

"If you decline this proposal, I'll deny this discussion ever happened. You'll be handed back to the Seattle Police Department, and any evidence that could prove you were defending yourself from muggers will disappear. And before you even ask, this is a limited-time deal."

So that was her angle. She hadn't even bothered to lean forward to punctuate her threat, but she didn't need to. She had me dead to rights, and she knew it. If I opted to let this go to trial, I stood a chance of losing everything and ending up in a cell for longer than I cared to think about. Without the video footage that showed me being dragged back into the alleyway, I had little hope of proving my innocence. Witnesses would say that I was drunk, and the muggers would probably claim that they were innocent of any crimes and that I had attacked them without provocation. I'd be hung out to dry.

"We're part of an organization that deals with supernatural problems, preferably before they come to the attention of mortals. If you agree to work with us, you'll become a consultant for the team and report to me or Feldman, depending on the circumstances."

"What kind of problems?" I'd finally got a word in, but I had a suspicion that I currently counted as one of those problems. I was screwed either way, but I had to know what I was getting myself into.

"You're probably aware that some supernatural elements cause trouble for mortals, willfully or otherwise. I've seen the file on you, Richard, and you've not led a trouble-free life. You work for me and prove yourself to be an asset, and I'll bury your criminal record where only I'll ever find it again." She adjusted her hair and looked me right in the eye. "It's not going to be an easy job. You'll be operating in secret, and there will be necessary lifestyle changes. That means cutting yourself off from people you know... and your bad habits."

"You've got this all worked out, haven't you?"

"Consider it a suspended sentence, with community service and a decent paycheck. Or I could give you back to the Seattle PD and let them process you through the usual channels." Her smile had returned, and I knew, without doubt, that this woman was the biggest predator in the room.

As if to hammer home her point, the screen started playing again, showing the moment that Officer Talbot was hit by the truck. I may have had reservations about joining her team, but I also felt guilty about what had happened.

Maybe I deserved to take whatever punishment the authorities would hand out and should suffer the...

No, I couldn't face the idea of being locked up for days, months, or even years. My wolf needed to run, to hunt. I couldn't do that from inside a jail cell, no matter how short my sentence was.

If I joined Cooperfield's team, I'd be living with a potential conflict of interest. I wouldn't be able to talk to anyone about what I did for a living, but if my few friends in the supernatural community were to find out, word would spread, and I'd be alienated.

To make matters worse, I wanted to talk to Nazurl or Art and get their advice. But if I spoke to Nazurl, she'd have to learn that I was a lupine, and I'd avoided that discussion for several reasons. As far as she knew, my semi-regular overnight camping trips were visits to friends or overnight stays in a rehab center. It was better to let her believe those lies than the fact that I went up into the mountains to hunt as a wolf.

I couldn't talk to Art because he'd try to talk me out of it. While our friendship was rocky, he'd always been there when I needed him. This would go against everything he stood for. He believed that the supernatural had to police themselves to remain hidden. And I'd be signing on with the agencies he avoided involving in pack business.

That left a couple of factors to consider...

"What about the muggers?"

"They'll live, unfortunately. However, they keep insisting that a drunken madman attacked them. And, given the damage you inflicted, even I'd be hard-pressed not to believe they were at least partially right."

That sealed it. The muggers would recover, while one of Seattle's decorated police officers died. I'd probably never be able to press charges for the attempted mugging because of my criminal record. It'd be the word of three victims and the Seattle PD against mine.

I didn't have a hope in hell...

I sighed and slumped back into the chair, letting the cold metal soothe me briefly. I closed my eyes and blocked out as many distractions as possible. I'd already thought through all the possibilities, so there was only one thing left to do...

I made the second worst decision of my life.

Chapter Five

January 12th, 2022

I raced across the asphalt of the covered parking lot next to the Silver Cloud Hotel, the stench of early morning exhaust fumes stinging my nostrils. I'd lost sight of my target, but there were only so many places for him to hide.

It was early in the day, many of the hotel's guests had already left, and there were fewer vehicles than I might have otherwise expected. As I passed each one, I glanced around to see if the vampire might have been hiding in the shadows, but I didn't pick up more than a trace of his scent. I hadn't heard any of the stairway doors closing, so I was sure he'd managed to find his way onto Broadway.

I quickly reviewed what I knew about my quarry, hoping to guess his next move. I had him on charges of assaulting a mortal woman and feeding off her, as well as property damage from where he'd broken into the parking lot.

I figured he was either a relatively new vampire or desperate because he'd attacked the woman in broad daylight and dragged her into an alleyway. This was not normal for his race, regardless of what sub-species he belonged to. It had also taken a lot of strength to rip that heavy wire mesh out of its housing, which wouldn't have been possible without a recent feeding.

He was also fast, possibly faster than me, but I knew the streets of Seattle like the back of my hand, and I was a born hunter.

I don't care what anyone tries to tell me; vampires are not natural hunters. They learn to hunt once they've been turned. Lupines, like me, are born with the hunt in our blood. It's part of our wolf nature; some who embrace our wild side can tap into those instincts and senses.

It was all the same to me, whether I was hunting him through the woods of Cougar Mountain or the city streets. I treated both the same way, as a series of twists, turns, obstacles, and conflicting scents.

My only goal was to make sure the vampire didn't get away to attack anyone else. Even though the supernatural community tended to police itself, some thought they could do a better job.

Unfortunately, I'd answered to those people over the last six months, not my own.

Damn! That reminded me that I was supposed to be taking part in a raid just off U-District, not chasing down a mugger. I'd have to radio in my status as soon as I had the opportunity.

As I sprinted for the early morning sunlight, I could hear heavy traffic on Broadway and the chatter of the morning commuters. That would complicate things because I didn't want to spook the vampire into making drastic moves. His ability to feed from his victims could further enhance his speed and strength, and I'd lose him in the crowds.

I had to force a mistake and somehow steer him out of the main flow of pedestrians.

I broke into the open air and blinked at the change in lighting conditions, holding my hand up to reduce the sun's glare as I looked around. I pulled my radio out of my pocket and called the dispatcher for the Supernatural Taskforce as I looked around.

I kept the volume turned down to try and avoid my prey overhearing the conversation. Even though I couldn't see him, I kept looking as I talked.

"Wolf-man to Dispatch. I'm pursuing a male vampire with blond hair and over six feet. The suspect mugged a mortal female. Requesting backup and medical assistance."

I gave the location where I'd left the victim while I waited for the dispatcher to get over the fact that I wasn't following radio protocol again and respond.

I looked left toward Madison, hoping I hadn't lost the vampire while trying to get assistance. I knew there was no way I could capture and detain him without help.

And that was when I spotted him again. Off to my left - that shock of bright blond hair was unmistakable. Of course, his height didn't help with blending into the crowds.

He was hustling along like he had to be somewhere urgently, not as though he was trying to escape pursuit. Thankfully, that meant he was only halfway between me and the junction of East Madison.

If I could navigate the crowd without him spotting me, I could probably catch him as he tried to cross the junction. I just had to figure out how to separate him from the crowd. I looked further ahead and realized what was on the other side of the road.

I got a wild idea.

I pulled my wallet out of my back pocket and flashed it at those around me, yelling, "Police, coming through." While the action drew a lot of attention to me, it allowed me to push my way through the crowd toward the oncoming traffic.

As I approached the corner, I faked a look across the street as if I thought I'd seen my quarry on the opposite side while checking the junction to my left. And just as I'd hoped, I saw my prey cross with the changing light and turn onto Madison.

I chose my moment carefully and pushed past a couple of people going in the opposite direction as I raced the changing light.

I made it onto East Madison just as my quarry looked back behind him.

He'd hoped to outmaneuver me, but as soon as he spotted me heading his way, he panicked and dived through the bushes that separated the Seattle University grounds from the street.

I knew from experience that the bushes weren't dense, so I pursued, breaking through onto the open lawn moments behind my prey.

After a glance around, I saw him trying to merge with a group of students heading toward the Garrand Building. I smiled as I waved at the group to get their attention.

"Hey, I'm trying to find the Casey Building," I called out as I approached. "I've got a meeting there, and I got turned around."

I couldn't make my move around civilians, so I joined the group as they headed deeper into the campus. Because I was worried for their safety, I settled on trying to make the vampire as uncomfortable as possible while I got directions from one of the students.

Sure enough, before I could extract myself from the group, my quarry was already looking for an opportunity to make a break for it. As we passed the corner of the parking structure, he darted along the side of the building, putting a few precious yards between us before I could respond.

The chase was on, and I wanted to howl with the ecstasy of it.

Wolves In The Desert (Prequels #3)

Chapter One

Mission Briefing

I looked across at the four-man fire team and reflected on how young a couple of them looked. But none of them would have made the team if they had not already proven themselves during boot camp. There was no place in the Corps for people who might buckle at the first sign of pressure, and I knew that each of them had already faced more during their training than most civilians would face in their entire lives.

Corporal Thomas Walters looked over at me as if reading my thoughts. He was good at that. He was good at reading people in general, and it was one of the things that made him a good team leader. To his left sat Private Ken Saki, one hell of a close-quarters fighter. Then one seat down came Stephen Bonander, our field radio operator, and the team's youngest member.

Sat to my right was Private First-Class Kaitlin Willenborg, our scout sniper. She was a sure shot with an M-16A2 automatic rifle due to her icy-cold and clinical demeanor. I had heard that Willenborg had had to push to get into sniper training but had been outshooting her instructors within a month. Willenborg also doubled as Bonander's tactical switching operator. In simple terms, she was his assistant and backup - an unusual combination of roles helped by her experience with her father's ham radio rig.

In a weird symbiotic partnership, Bonander functioned as her spotter. During a cross-training exercise, they had built up chemistry, and he was the only person she trusted to provide clicks and windage information. I didn't question it, because they worked so well together.

There was a little chatter from the other marines in the transport, and I liked it that way. I had two other fire teams in my squad, but for the moment, there was no sense in worrying too much about them. They would be joining us as soon as we arrived at our destination.

Someone had decided to split each squad into their constituent fire teams and put each team on separate transports. While it may have seemed like a crazy idea, it at least kept the fire teams themselves together. There is nothing worse than breaking a team into parts, losing members of that team, and trying to build a new team on the fly. It had been done, and top-class training and discipline made it possible, but not desirable.

I looked behind me, trying to figure out which of the other transports my other squad members might be on. Unfortunately, the roads were so dusty with wind-blown sand that it was hard to see much past the first five trucks.

There were three trucks ahead of us and one about a half mile ahead of them. The lead truck in this convoy was our pace vehicle, our eyes and ears on the road ahead, and the one in the most danger. The enemy had taken to placing explosive devices along the local roads, sometimes hidden in bodies, and set with tripwires, motion sensors, or even remote triggers. Over the last few months, our forces had lost several vehicles and soldiers to this tactic.

There was no sense looking back on what had already happened, but it did give every one of us an idea of what our enemies were capable of. I turned back to my fire team and gave them my usual prepared speech.

"Okay devil dogs, listen up. The enemy is probably expecting us. Our dust cloud has probably announced our arrival by now. If we're lucky, they won't have much time to get word to the Fedayeen Saddam forces, and we won't be facing an organized opposition. People in the houses and streets are most likely going to be civilians. This is a sweep-and-capture mission. We have several confirmed target locations, and there are likely to be more. I want everyone to confirm the status of potential targets before engaging. I don't want any civilian casualties on our tally. So, eyes open, ears unplugged, and be careful. I don't want anyone to make any assumptions. Any questions?"

I smiled as Walters raised his hand. I nodded, even though I knew I was probably going to regret it. Or end up laughing.

"Yeah, Gunny. Will you take a sick note from my momma?"

I had to keep the smile off my face. I could always trust Walters to break the tension before a mission, but we were heading into enemy territory, and I needed my people sharp.

"Cut it out, Walters. I can always have you busted down to Lance Corporal." I paused to let that sink in. "Now, do you have any mission-related questions?"

Willenborg brought us back to the matter at hand: "What kind of armaments are we likely to be encountering? How fortified are our key targets? Are the enemy organized or disjointed?"

"From aerial surveillance, we are likely facing small arms, personal artillery, and the usual range of explosive devices. Keep an eye out for tripwires, decoys, and rigged bodies. If you are unable to tell if an object is booby-trapped, I don't want you playing hero. Secure the area, and get it checked. Fortifications are likely to be light, but the enemy knows these buildings and streets, so make no assumptions about where an enemy might fire from."

As the transport pulled up at the city walls, several enemy positions opened fire. Our snipers took cover while spotters tried to find the shooters and called out the necessary ranges and bearings. Within a few short moments, the number of incoming rounds was dramatically reduced, and the order came through to advance.

I gestured for my Beta and Charlie teams to join me for a moment, and we hunkered down behind one of the transports while I gave them a quick briefing.

"Okay, Marines, we have minimal enemy contact at the moment. If anyone out there decides to bring out an RPG we are going to have zero cover. With that in mind, I want a loose formation as we head in. Watch windows and doors for snipers and take them out quickly."

I got a rousing acknowledgment from all sides and remembered why I'd picked these people. They were among the best available. They'd trained, worked, and played together for months. There were very few squads out there that were as closely knit as mine, and they made me proud to lead them.

It was a tradition in my squad to take a moment for prayer, so I closed my eyes and started to mutter the Lord's Prayer under my breath. As I did, I heard Dalessandro of Charlie team mumble something in Stermbach's ear, and I raised my eyes to them both.

"What was that, Dalessandro? I didn't quite catch that."

He looked back at me, a little sheepish, "I said, I hear they're strapping bombs on their dogs and kids."

"If they are, then you shoot the dog and avoid hitting the explosive. If it's a child, you clear the area and call in a bomb expert. If you find anyone armed, they are a potential target; hold fire until you're sure. If they attack or offer violence, then consider them a legitimate target. They are to be captured where possible or eliminated if necessary."

I gave them a moment to digest the information and then gestured for them to move out. Leading my team toward the walls, I reflected quickly on other rumors that I'd heard and dismissed them from my mind. There was no point dwelling on what other people had reported seeing, especially when there was no way those stories could be true.

Chapter Two

Firefight

As soon as we passed through the city wall, I directed Charlie and Beta teams down the streets to our left and right while I took my team straight down the middle. Other teams were deployed into the streets further down as we made our way toward the market square in the city center.

Surrounded by dry stone walls and narrow alleyways, the area could have become very claustrophobic if the streets had been busier. We passed only a handful of civilians since most were huddled in their homes, trying to avoid getting mixed up in our search.

As we moved deeper into the city, we searched homes and businesses with precision. A few times, we heard the eruption of gunfire from nearby streets, followed by radio calls reporting successful kills or captures. A smaller handful of reports came in letting us know that enemy shooters had been seen leaving an area and that we should be on the lookout, though most of those were outside our designated search zone.

My teams got lucky, and for the most part, we encountered little more than scared civilians and empty buildings. Because it had proved so quiet in our search grid, I suspected that something unusual might be going on and ordered everyone to keep a wary eye out for trouble.

About an hour into our search, I saw Bonander put a finger to his earpiece and request a repeat of the incoming report.

"Sir, Beta team reports... " his words were drowned out by the chatter of automatic weapon fire in the near distance. "... sniper fire, three streets down. Charlie team is moving in to assist".

I nodded my understanding and then heard a muffled explosion in the opposite direction. Since there were no follow-up reports, I had to assume that no one had been injured and made my plan accordingly.

"Okay. We're going to give Beta and Charlie teams some support. We are going to find those snipers and remove them from the fight. Understood?"

I nodded to Bonander, and he pointed in the direction Beta team had reported the encounter. Right into the heart of that automatic fire, we'd heard as the report came in.

We made about fifteen yards before Bonander received another report, amid even more gunfire and explosions, this time much closer than before.

"Charlie team reporting intense enemy fire. Automatic weapons, and at least one RPG."

We turned into an alley ahead, and the sounds of gunfire diminished as the buildings closed in around us. I gestured to pick up the pace, and we raced toward our fellow squad members. I just hoped we weren't too late to be of assistance.

Every member of the team was scanning the path ahead or watching for potential snipers from the windows high over our heads. That meant we weren't caught off guard by the three men with dogs who entered the far end of the alley and blocked our exit route.

I signaled to my fellow team members to halt so we could assess the situation. Every single one of us was on high alert, as I stepped forward to inquire if they intended to resist our progress. I had managed to close about half the distance between our two groups when their leader raised a shotgun from behind his leg and started to swing it around to aim at me.

My team reacted instantly, splitting up almost as soon as the shotgun came into sight. Each of them moved as part of a well-coordinated whole, heading for cover or better firing positions. I dropped to the ground, keeping my eyes on both the gunman and the dog handlers.

The first shots were already in the air as the gunman tried to get a bead on me, and several rounds hit him in the chest, sending him backward. His yelps of pain suggested that he was probably wearing body armor under his civvies and that he was probably not out of the fight just yet.

At a whistled command, the entire pack of dogs accelerated toward my team, barking and snarling, ready for a fight. From my prone position, I was very aware of those sharp teeth closing in on me and found myself grateful for the layers of body armor designed to withstand slashing and stabbing attacks.

In under a second, I had one of the dogs barreling into me, trying to charge me down again, as I started rising to my feet. Had I not crouched, the tactic might have worked, but thankfully, my center of gravity was low enough that I was able to put a hand down and only get knocked back a little. I rolled backward and thrust hard with my legs, planting my feet into the beast's belly. I used its momentum against it and threw it several feet behind me.

I scrambled around to face the creature, trying to watch my men at the same time, and realized that the dogs were fighting individual targets. Teeth bit into the straps holding armor in place, and claws tried to rake around the edges of plates to strike exposed areas.

I didn't have time to see much more than that as I heard a loud gunshot from somewhere nearby, and my head started ringing. I lost sight of the dog that had attacked me, but that wouldn't matter if the gunman and handlers entered the fight too.

I heard a scream of agony and saw one of the dogs had its teeth locked around Bonander's thigh and was trying to tear out a chunk of meat. Despite the pain, he kicked hard. Managing to throw the dog, he watched it carefully as he listened intently to the radio chatter.

"Charlie team reports that they are holed up in..."

The dog charged back in, but Bonander was already drawing his knife and met the attack with a quick slice, forcing the dog to veer off sharply or risk a fatal injury. As the dog circled, Bonander kept up his report on the progress of the other teams, between grunts of pain and his own attacks and counterattacks.

"... a house. Snipers have ceased... ceased fire, but dogs are prowling... ...the streets. I heard barking on Beta..."

He opened fire with his sidearm, as the dog tried to jump him, and he went down under its dead weight. It took a few moments for him to roll the body off, get his breath back, and continue his report.

"... team's channel, and now they've gone silent... What the hell are we facing here, sergeant?"

I didn't have time to answer the Private's question, as the dog handlers fired their semi-automatics, sending rounds down the alleyway in quick bursts. The dogs backed off, as if at some prearranged signal, and we tried to take cover from the incoming hail of hot metal.

I saw Bonander stumble, as he made for one of the walls, and then his head snapped backward, and I knew without even checking that he wasn't going to be making any further reports.

I saw Saki and Walters try to make their way across the alley, ducking low to present smaller targets for our enemies, but the dogs were circling back in. I ordered them back into cover until I could come up with a way to get us all out of this alive. Three gunmen and three dogs stood between us and the remaining members of my squad. Those squad members were in trouble too, and it looked like I was going to need help getting out of this mess.

I had to get to that radio, so we could call for aid, but I could only see one way to do it. I rotated the selector switch on my M-16 to full auto, yelled for my team to stay down, and dove out of cover. Bullets sprayed down the alleyway behind me as I tried to make my way back toward the rest of my team and Bonander's body.

The movies lie when they show this kind of thing happening in slow motion. I had no concept of where those bullets were flying, and only the vaguest impression of managing to hit something with my shoulder as I flew into one of the dogs, Bonander's body, and finally the hard dust-covered ground.

I flailed around, using everything at my disposal to drive the dogs away from Bonander's body. A couple of shots landed close, as my team tried to keep the dogs off my back.

Then, I was staring down one of those beasts and caught a glimpse of dangerous intelligence and understanding in those eyes. I put my hand down to brace myself and found it landing on the radio unit. With my goal in hand, I threw my entire weight forward, butting my thick helmet into the beast's muzzle, and heard a satisfying crunch and yelp of pain. I followed up by shoving my pistol against its throat and put it out of its misery.

I ripped the radio free and nodded to my team to continue firing. The noise was deafening as we unleashed hell on that alleyway, and I was hard-pressed to reach the platoon commander.

I listened closely to the orders and repeated them for the benefit of my squad. There was a lump in my throat as I realized that we had lost this engagement.

"Pull back, pick targets with care. Conserve your ammo. All targets considered hostile. Rendezvous at the secondary extraction point".

I kept firing as I rose to my feet and took a couple of steps backward toward my team. The enemy was taking advantage of the same cover we had previously used, and my bullets missed every target. I had to yell to be heard over the sound of barking and gunfire.

"Find a way back to the evac point. I'll cover the retreat."

Chapter Three

Devil Dogs

My feet moved, and I conserved ammunition by only firing at targets that presented themselves, and we soon reached where we had entered the alleyway. Willenborg started firing over my head as Saki pulled around the corner, and Saki's pistol barked a couple of times from the other side of the opening.

Willenborg and I covered the alleyway, allowing Saki to rejoin us. I sent him and Walters to scout the way ahead while I prepared a little surprise for any pursuit. I grabbed grenades from my belt and Willenborg's, pulled the pins, and ducked far enough around the corner to throw them down the alleyway. I caught glimpses of clothing being ripped off as the gunmen stripped themselves bare.

Then, as the grenades arced high, I saw something I hoped never to see again. The forms of the gunmen were melting, shifting into something else, as they dropped to all fours, tails extending back from their spines. I must have frozen in shock because the next thing I knew, we were all racing down the street, and Willenborg was pulling me by the front of my fatigues.

We raced through the broader streets, barking and canine yapping from all sides. If I hadn't seen what was happening to the gunmen back in that alleyway, I'd have assumed we were dealing with nothing more than a very well-trained pack of dogs. But it was far worse than that. Our enemy was intelligent and all too human. How does one fight creatures of myth, legend, and horror films?

Occasional shots rang out from sniper positions as we tried to shake our pursuers. Taking turns at random, we made for the city's outskirts, but the creatures kept getting closer. Several times, we had to fight off attacks from side alleys as the enemy coordinated against us, and before long, I watched Willenborg taken down by a pack of monsters. I fired into the melee several times, hoping to take out some of the enemy, but I was rapidly running out of ammunition. There were too many of them, and I ordered Saki and Walters to keep moving as I threw another grenade behind me, knowing that I had already lost my second marine.

I tried to radio my other teams, advise them of our position, and arrange a rendezvous point, but I received only static in response. This meant one of two things: either they were too busy to respond or could not respond. I hoped they'd only met with Fedayeen Saddam forces; at least they were human. Whatever we had run into was far from it.

After several failed communication attempts, I had to allow for the possibility that my fire team was all that was left of the squad. I would be sure to find out what happened to them because I would be answerable to my superiors, the families of those lost marines, and myself.

Saki was the next to drop, and mercifully, it was to a sniper's round rather than those unearthly beasts. Walters and I tried to strip the ammunition off Saki's body as the sniper took shots at us, but we had to abandon our attempts as the dogs closed in on us.

Every time the snipers became active, the dogs backed off their pursuit, and I realized that they were trying to drive us parallel to the city walls instead of toward them. This suggested that the entire city had been used as a carefully laid trap, baited with the appearance of minor enemy activity while hiding the true nature of our enemy. The dogmen were intended to either kill us or drive us back toward the ring of snipers hidden inside the city walls. The organization that went into an operation like this was staggering, yet surveillance showed no sign of it. Either something was rotten about the intel, or they'd withheld information on the true nature of the enemy troops. I know it wouldn't have been something I'd have believed. I'd seen it but still wasn't sure I believed it.

Walters and I braved the sniper fire, and I was the first to break through the city walls. With the trucks in sight, I yelled for Walters to get his backside in gear and get to one of the transports. He'd been behind me moments before, but now I saw nothing like he'd never even existed.

I made for the truck as fast as I could, watching as marines emptied their magazines into the dogs pouring out of the city. I counted maybe twenty, then thirty, before I stopped counting, threw myself into the back of a truck, and turned to fire behind me.

I stopped when I saw Dalessandro and another marine break cover from an archway and try to pick their way across the open sand toward my truck. Both bore numerous wounds and supported each other's weight as if it were the only way they could keep moving.

I reached down and helped them board as I heard Command issue the order to pull everything out of there before they blanketed the place with bombs. Someone had finally made some sense of the situation and was going to deal with it.

Seconds later, the first of the bombers flew overhead and dropped several tons of mayhem on the city. With luck, those monsters would be caught in the explosions and fires, but somehow, I doubted this was the last I would see of those creatures.

Appointment With Death (Prequels #4)

Chapter One

Break-In - October 31st, 2020

This is the report of Officer Agneta Dottasen, West Precinct of the Seattle Police Department.

At approximately twenty-thirty hours, I was on Queen Anne Avenue North, listening to the radio chatter between dispatch and other units. My partner, Officer James McClaren, was out sick, so I rode solo with Lieutenant Reilly's reluctant permission.

I was returning to the precinct after following up on a phone call from one of my informants. It turned out he'd been drinking again, and his story held together about as well as a piece of tissue paper in a bowl of acid. I told him he'd be in hot water the next time he called to waste police time.

I'd just turned south onto Queen Anne when a message from dispatch came over the channel.

"Dispatch to all mobile units. We have a possible zero-fifty-two in progress at the McCaw Museum, on the corner of Fourth and Mercer."

A zero-fifty-two meant a non-residential burglary, which could mean that one or more display pieces were stolen. Had the burglar broken in last month, they would have been able to grab several sculptures, some of which had been valued in the hundreds of thousands of dollars range.

However, I happened to know that there wasn't anything famous or of value on display. The McCaw only housed traveling exhibitions, and they were currently playing host to recreations of local wildlife in their natural environments. Some of the animals had been caught, stuffed, and mounted, while all that remained of others were their pelts.

I toured the exhibits just a couple of days ago, and they were an exciting collection. What impressed me most was that each of the animals in the display had a reference sheet that gave details of how and where they had been killed or died. One display caught my attention because it included two creatures I hadn't thought about when considering predators in the Washington area.

In hindsight, their presence should have been obvious.

The centerpiece showed two hunters with rifles, hidden in the underbrush, waiting to shoot a mother wolf and her cub. Just imagining the potential outcome of that scene sent a shiver down my spine even now.

I couldn't imagine what a burglar might have been after from the collection, but I was curious enough to want to know. I was also close by, so I decided to take the call from dispatch and investigate. I grabbed my radio from the passenger seat and hit the talk button.

"Ten-four dispatch. This is car twenty. I'm southbound on Queen Anne, approaching Galer. I can be onsite in five."

"Ten-twelve car twenty." I'd been put on hold, so I assumed the dispatcher was checking on the locations of other officers in the area before giving me the go-ahead to investigate. "Ten-Four car twenty. Please proceed to that zero-five-two. Patrol officers en route to assist, Lieutenant Reilly's orders."

I smiled to myself. Reilly had always been a little protective of his officers, especially some of the more recent recruits. I'd have stern words with him when I returned to the precinct. He knew I was more than capable of handling myself.

"Ten-four dispatch. I'll rendezvous with patrol on site. Has anyone spoken to the museum staff?"

It might have been an obvious question, but I asked it anyway. I wanted to be sure that this wasn't a prank call from a bored college kid or someone trying to garner interest for the exhibition.

"That's a negative, car twenty. We're still trying to reach museum security or senior staff."

"Let me know if anything changes, dispatch. Car twenty out."

I'd continued driving toward the McCaw Museum while talking to dispatch because the longer it took an officer to reach the site, the more chance we had of losing the burglar. I'd lost a few suspects because it took too long to respond to a call, and I never liked losing to criminals. I turned my lights on and hit the siren to let people know I was responding to an urgent call. I raced through the turn onto Mercer Street.

I left the lights running as I pulled over about half a block from the McCaw Museum, grabbed my radio, locked the doors, and started heading toward the building. I was about halfway there when a side door opened, and I saw one of the patrol officers coming out. He was talking on his radio when he spotted me and waved.

I smiled and waved back. Recognizing Jon Masters wasn't too hard. We'd worked together ever since I'd joined the West Precinct. Slowing my pace as I approached, I waited for Masters to finish his report before saying hi.

"Hey Agneta, I wondered who dispatch was sending over to deal with the pickup on this one. Must admit, it's always good seeing you, Red."

He'd been calling me that from day one because of my bright red hair, and somehow, from him, I didn't mind it. If it had been anyone else, I'd have been having words. I was curious to know more about the break-in, but this was Masters' collar, so I let him take his time.

As he was about to speak, his radio squawked. "Roger that, Masters. I'll let mobile know".

He looked back at me with a smile as he thumbed the radio. "Ten-ten, dispatch. Mobile has just arrived. I'll let her know."

"Let me know what?" I asked, and I looked back toward the open door, expecting Jon's partner to bring out a prisoner. Instead, she came out empty-handed.

"Hey Taft, where's your prisoner?"

"Would you believe it was a false alarm? The night guard says she has no idea who called it in, and she'd just completed a full walk of the interior when dispatch reached her."

"Any chance she's lying to cover for someone?" I knew the thought had probably already crossed his mind because Masters had the kind of mind that worked that way. But he was also a good judge of character, so I knew I trusted him when he told me he'd ruled out that possibility.

"In that case, Jon, I'd better see what else dispatch has on the cards for me. I'll catch you both back at the precinct, and you can fill me in if anything changes on this one."

Chapter Two

First Responder

Before climbing back into the cruiser, I looked back toward my colleagues. Masters and Taft were talking to the museum's night guard. Whatever they were discussing must have been amusing because I saw Masters laughing. I almost wished I could join in, but I was relegated to supporting regular patrol officers without my partner riding along. And that meant getting back on the road.

I opened the door of my vehicle as I radioed dispatch. "Car twenty to dispatch."

"Go ahead, car twenty." The dispatcher sounded tired, but then she was probably coming to the end of her shift. It wasn't an easy job because they filtered many incoming calls and sorted out which required a response, and which didn't.

"McCaw museum was a ten forty, so what have you got for me next?" I smiled as I spoke, trying to make the end of the shift a little easier.

That tiredness seemed to kick up a notch as the response came back, "We have a ten fifty-seven on the corner of Broad and Second. The caller is barely coherent, and Patrol cannot respond promptly."

I looked at the traffic as I climbed into the cruiser and buckled up. I was already pulling out into traffic, with my lights and siren running, as I continued to talk to the dispatcher. "Ten-four dispatch. I have some traffic ahead on Fifth, but if you can green light me all the way, I can be there in less than a couple of minutes."

It was an unusual request to make, but with a hit-and-run accident, there could be lives hanging in the balance.

"Ten-four car twenty. I'll notify traffic control. Report any sightings of a dark grey sedan loitering near the scene. Three other units are inbound to assist but will be at least a couple of minutes behind your arrival."

The dispatcher knew as well as I did that sometimes the drivers involved in a hit-and-run drove away because they were worried about getting in trouble or already were. But some stopped near the incident scene because their guilt wouldn't let them drive away without learning what happened. Fewer still returned to the scene so they could see first-hand what was happening in the aftermath of the accident.

It was human nature to fear the consequences, but if the driver was anywhere in the area, we had to take them in for fleeing the scene. But right now, that wasn't my primary concern. I was already turning off Fifth Avenue toward the Space Needle and was maybe five or six blocks from the accident.

Knowing that foot traffic around the Space Needle was likely slight, I put my foot down. I kept a close eye on the sidewalks and junctions, not wanting to cause another RTA.

"Ten-four dispatch. Car twenty out."

Thankfully, the combination of siren and lights must have been enough to warn people of my presence, and I slowed as I approached the corner of Second Avenue.

Pulling in behind the growing crowd, I was sickened by the morbid curiosity that seemed to drive some people. I revved the engine on the cruiser, trying to let people know I was there, but none of them seemed inclined to move, so I hit the siren and started to pull forward slowly. Finally, the stragglers at the back of the crowd seemed to notice me, clearing the way for me to advance a little closer to whatever had their attention.

It took maybe thirty seconds for the last of the crowd to disperse enough for me to pull the cruiser into the junction. I turned the cruiser side-on, blocking access to the scene from Broad Street. There was enough space front and back to enable other mobile units to pass if needed.

I climbed out of the cruiser and got my first look at the accident. A motorbike lay off to one side, facing the wrong direction, and there was no sign of the rider. At first glance, it didn't look too bad until I started to follow the skid mark back toward where the impact must have occurred.

Pieces of fiberglass formed a trail between where the bike went down and finally stopped. They were most likely parts of the cowl and fairings, shorn off by the impact or as the bike scraped over the tarmac. From where I was, I couldn't tell if any of the debris was from the car that had hit the bike, but it didn't matter. I had to find the rider and make sure he was okay.

But where to start looking?

I tried to do a quick reconstruction of the accident in my head. Based on the debris and the state of the bike, I knew that the impact had probably happened on the front right quadrant. The second set of skid marks showed which way the car was traveling at the time of impact, and I was surprised to see that they were turning from Broad Street onto Second. That suggested they had hit the bike on the right front side, pushing it across the street and back down Second toward Clay Street.

It wasn't too hard to locate the rider because two pedestrians were waving at me. They stood in front of a parked vehicle on the other side of the road. Now that my attention had been drawn in that direction, I could see the boot and hand sticking out from around a parked SUV. No doubt they belonged to the victim.

I raced across the street as the first of my backups arrived on the scene. I had to trust that they'd close off the area while I attempted to ascertain the situation with the biker.

"Car twenty to dispatch. Requesting a ten-fifty-two at that ten-fifty-seven on Broad and Second. Biker down, possible injuries. I'm investigating now."

"Ten-four car twenty. EMTs have been listening in. I have a confirmed unit inbound to your location."

As I approached the front of the SUV, I saw the biker lying there while an older woman spoke to him in a calm, soothing voice. I was thankful that the rider had been wearing a helmet, but I could tell there had been a significant impact because the visor had cracks running through it. Somehow, it had held up through the collision and following events.

I did a quick visual assessment of the biker and realized he was not much older than his early twenties. The angle of the left leg showed that it had been broken and quite possibly in more than one place. Despite the helmet, I suspected a concussion was also likely. However, there was little I could see through the thick layers of leather and padding he was wearing.

The only big question I had was whether there were any internal injuries, and I wasn't going to be able to learn anything more without an assessment from the EMTs. In the meantime, I had to do whatever I could for the young man until the medical team arrived.

Getting down on my knees, I leaned in to talk to the biker. But a hand on my arm stopped me from leaning in too far, and I glanced around to see who was there. Looking around at the older lady, I searched her eyes for anything she might have heard. But she kept her expression neutral, and I couldn't get a read on her. I almost asked her to remove the hand, but there was a gentle reassurance in that touch, and I suddenly didn't have the heart to ask.

I leaned forward again and reached out to try to lift the biker's visor when I felt that hand squeeze my arm. She was shaking her head at me, and her eyes had a sadness that hadn't been there before.

I looked at her again, and only then did I see her nurse's uniform under the heavy jacket. She probably had a better idea of her patient's condition than I did, but I still wanted to assure them that help was coming.

I didn't reach for the visor again as I spoke. "Hey there. I'm Agneta Dottasen with the SPD. I know you're probably in a lot of pain right now, but we have EMTs on the way. I need you to lie still for me, okay?"

The words came in a whisper, interspersed by quiet coughs, and I had to lean close to hear them. "Sure, officer. It's not like I can move much anyway."

I took his gloved hand in mine as I talked. He sounded so weak and scared despite the attempt at humor. And that coughing had me worried that there might have been cracked ribs or even internal bleeding.

"What's your name, kid?"

Beside me, I could see the nurse fingering the beads on a rosary, and her lips moved in silent prayer. And I joined her in one of my own – hoping that the EMTs would get here in time to save this young man's life.

"Morris, James Morr..." His words were cut off by another coughing fit, and I worried he might be doing more internal damage. I held his hand through it all, feeling slightly uncomfortable but hoping it comforted him.

"Where were you heading, James?"

"Costume shop. I needed something for the party." His words and breathing seemed to be getting slower, and I could see he was trying to fight through the pain to answer me. But I had to keep him talking because if he did have a concussion, keeping him conscious was important.

I pushed his visor up so he could see me more clearly, and I looked down at his pained features. I finally saw just how much pain he was in, but there was a spark of something defiant in his eyes as he fought to stay with us. How he was still conscious, I had no idea because even with what little I could see, it was clear that he'd taken at least one severe blow to the side of the head.

At this point, it didn't matter when the damage had been done, but the helmet might have been the only thing that had stopped the wound from being immediately fatal. Instead, it had provided just enough padding to prolong his suffering.

I tried to put a smile on my face for him. "I have a feeling you'll have to miss the party." It seemed like such a stupid thing to say at the time, but he gave me a weak smile.

"Yeah, looks that wa...." was the last thing he said to me, as I listened for the next breath. It never came.

I felt the beginning of tears as the old nurse pulled me onto her shoulder and slowly, gently pried my hand from James'. "Do you hear those sirens, dearie?" she asked me quietly, and I realized that I'd been so caught up in keeping our patient talking that I hadn't heard the ambulance pull up.

Gentle hands pulled me onto the sidewalk as the EMTs got to work. "Let them do their job, sweetie. This your first fatality?"

I couldn't even answer as the tears poured from me, my body shaking with shock. Thoughts raced through my mind, only to get lost, found, and lost all over again in the jumble of emotions that I usually held so carefully in check. Even if anyone asked me, I wouldn't have been able to tell them why this boy's death hit me as hard as it did. But, in those short moments of conversation, he'd somehow kept hoping despite everything.

***

The next few minutes passed in a haze, and I was barely even aware of the EMTs or other officers until someone from patrol came to check on me.

I felt a hand on my shoulder and looked up into Cecelia Taft's face. The nurse pulled away from me, leaving me in the care of my fellow officers, but I made a mental note to get her name so I could arrange to thank her for the kindness she had shown me. I almost didn't want to let go, but I knew I still had a job to do and reports to write up.

"Hey Dottasen. You don't look so good."

That was probably an understatement, but I was grateful for the woman's company. I barely knew her, except as Jon's beat partner, but there's a connection between fellow officers that few outside the force could ever understand.

If we were lucky, we'd reach retirement age without looking back on our time in the service and seeing only the worst things people did to each other. That's if we reached retirement age at all. Going through the academy, we'd been told that the rate of suicide among officers and ex-officers was higher than average. Today, I was getting an idea why. Morris had been barely any younger than I was, maybe three or four years at most. And now, he was just another statistic in a report I would have to write up.

"He was too young, Cecelia. Too young and too full of hope." I swallowed back another round of tears, "It shouldn't have happened like this."

Taft settled down beside me, and a blanket materialized from somewhere. She wrapped it around my shoulders, and I pulled the ends together against the shivers. I knew I was potentially going into shock and that I needed to get my anxiety back under control. There was too much still to do before I could go home and let myself fall apart entirely.

It suddenly hit me again, and Taft just sat there with me and held my hands as I cried out the last of my tears. It wasn't until I was dry and drained that I wondered where Masters was. Over the time I'd known him, he'd always brought me back to myself. The one who helped me back to that calm center I held inside to keep away the emotions that so often fought to overwhelm me.

"Get me out of here," I whispered, still trying to control the anxiety and knowing that I needed a change of scenery before that could happen.

Taft looked at me and nodded before pushing herself up. She stood over me, offering her hand, as I tried to get up. Somehow, in the short minutes I'd been sitting down, my legs had turned to jelly, and I had to lean against my fellow officer. Not exactly my most auspicious moment.

"Where are your keys?" It took me a few seconds to think. As I patted down my pockets and belt, it occurred to me that I probably hadn't even taken them out of the ignition. That was unlike me, but this shift was far from my usual routine.

"Ignition," I said as I stumbled back toward where I'd left the cruiser, slowly regaining the feeling and strength in my legs. Being on the move always seemed to help me recover at least a shred of control.

I let Taft steer me toward the passenger seat and had to move the seat back a little so that I could stretch my legs. Being able to breathe deeply kept my anxiety to a manageable level. But I knew I would have some meditation to do before I would be in a condition to sleep.

Chapter Three
A Sense Of Duty

The journey back to the precinct passed in a haze, and even though Taft and I kept talking, I couldn't recall a single moment of that conversation.

I left the blanket in the cruiser's passenger seat as we pulled into the parking lot. I would have to remember to fold it and put it in the trunk until I figured out who it belonged to.

Taft climbed out of the driver's side and threw me the keys. They bounced off my hand, and I caught them on the second attempt. My hands were a little shaky, but I had work to do now that we were back at the precinct. I was thankful that all the reports had to be typed because I didn't trust that my handwriting would be readable, but that wasn't a change from the usual.

I looked over at my colleague and was about to open my mouth to thank her when she cut me off with a wave of her hand.

"Don't mention it. Just promise you'll meet Jon and me for drinks after the shift. Okay?"

I was hesitant to accept the invitation, partly because I didn't drink but mostly because I'm not the most social creature. I found social occasions uncomfortable and avoided even spending time with my partner. Working with him was just fine because that was business. But I'd turned down enough invitations to social events that he eventually stopped asking.

Then again, I did owe Taft for being there when I needed someone and suppressed a sigh. "Sure. Where?"

"How about that bar down by headquarters?"

"Give me a couple of hours to finish the report, okay?"

Taft smiled as she nodded. She knew as well as I did that I wouldn't need that long. But I didn't give her a chance to respond as I headed inside, pocketing my keys.

A few conversations stopped as several sets of eyes turned my way, and I had to avert my eyes or take in those looks of sympathy. There weren't many of us who'd had to attend to the dying, but those who had would know precisely how I felt right now.

It took me around an hour to write up all the reports for the day, and it was the last one that got me thinking. I headed up to Lieutenant Reilly's office. I'd been the first on the scene of the traffic accident, and I had a question for him. Getting the correct answer was very important to me.

As always, the office door was open when I arrived, but I gave a courtesy knock anyway. Even though Reilly held to his open-door policy, most of us considered it rude to walk in without announcing ourselves first.

The Lieutenant looked up from his paperwork and waved me in. "I was wondering when I'd be seeing you, Dottasen. Any news on McClaren's condition?"

Apparently, this would be an informal discussion, so I settled into a comfortable standing position. I also stopped mentally rehearsing the conversation I'd been expecting to have and switched tracks. "No, sir. Although, knowing James, he'll try to return to work before he fully recovers."

"Leaving you to pick up the slack, eh?" He finally stood and pointed for me to take the only other seat in his office, directly opposite his own. "So, what can I do for you?"

I eased myself into the seat, feeling tired and stiff in most of my muscles. I've had workouts that left me feeling more exhausted than I was at that moment, but I couldn't avoid the reason for my visit any longer.

"I might need a favor, depending on the answer to a question." My wording was deliberate because I knew what I wanted to ask could be considered a delicate matter.

"You want to know if anyone has contacted the next of kin for that RTA kid?" I wasn't surprised that word had reached him about that incident. Reilly didn't miss much that happened during his watch, and I had a feeling he'd been keeping tabs on me since my partner wasn't riding along with me.

I nodded and kept silent. Considering the question, my favor seemed all too obvious. However, we sat there in silence for what felt like an eternity, but it was probably no more than a few seconds at most.

Finally, Reilly broke that silence with a slight nod and a quiet tone. The concern in his eyes was evident as he asked his question: " Are you sure you want to do this, Agneta? I can have a neighborhood officer do the visit."

"Yeah, I know that. But for some reason, I feel I owe It to James Morris. His folks deserve to hear about their son from someone who was there and can maybe answer any questions they have."

It wasn't precisely protocol for an attending officer to contact the family directly, but something deep down inside insisted that I had to be the one to make this visit. As part of my report, I'd pulled up Morris' record, and apart from a speeding violation, his record was clean. He was a good kid that something shitty happened to. What I'd told Reilly was the truth. I felt that I owed him and his family this one thing. It wouldn't bring him back, but it might just give them and me a little comfort to know that I'd done everything I could in his final moments.

The Lieutenant stood again and nodded. "There's no way I can persuade you to change your mind? You're already shaken up by all this, and the family will go through a lot of emotions very quickly."

"I know that sir," I said, pushing myself out of the seat, with only a slight shakiness to express how nervous I was about it. "I just think it's the right thing to do in this instance."

"Leave your car here. You're in no state to drive right now. I'll have someone drive you over there. And when you're done with the family, take the rest of the shift off. But, if you need to talk, you know where to find me."

I gave a small smile, and that took as much energy as I could summon. "Thank you, sir. I'll keep that in mind." Not that I had any intention of accepting the offer, especially with my therapist only a phone call away. I turned to leave the office, thinking the conversation was over for the moment, but I heard Reilly shuffling paperwork into a desk drawer and locking it.

"Dottasen, wait. Let me grab my keys, and I'll meet you in the parking lot." It might have been Reilly being overprotective again, but I appreciated the gesture and gave him a nod of acknowledgment.

Chapter Four

More Things In Heaven And Earth...

Reilly and I drove through Lower Queen Anne and turned toward Kerry Park. We pulled up outside some apartments on Comstock, and Reilly left the doors locked a moment longer.

His hand reached out for mine as he looked over at me. I could see the concern in his attempt at a smile. "I'll be down here if you need me." He gave my hand a quick squeeze before letting go. "It sounds like there's a party going on somewhere in the block. Consider yourself off the clock even if they get a little rowdy."

I wanted to reach out for the warmth of that hand to show my appreciation for his concern, but it would have been inappropriate. "Yes, sir. And thank you for this. It means a lot that you'd be here for me."

"You're a good officer, Dottasen. I've seen how things like this affect some people, and I don't want to lose someone with your promise."

I quickly nodded, reassuring Reilly that I could get through this, and headed for the apartments.

Approaching the entryway, I couldn't find an apartment index or buzzers. At least I had an apartment number. Pushing the door open, I was grateful to see signs that showed which apartments were on the first floor and which were on the remaining floors. I heard Thriller playing from somewhere upstairs, and a trail of giant footprints marked a route that went upstairs.

Two flights up, the prints turned off the stairs and onto the landing, leading to a door covered in webs and other Halloween decorations. As I reached out to knock on the door, Vincent Price was coming to the end of his guest piece at the end of the track. The moment I knocked, that iconic laugh rang out, and I almost jumped back, shocked by the timing.

I had to knock a couple more times before anyone answered the door, and this time I did jump.

After the day I'd had and the reason for my visit, the last thing I had expected to see was the tall, black-robed figure that greeted me. The apartment number matched the one I had from Morris' file, and it looked like I was about to ruin the party mood.

As it opened the door, I spotted the scythe resting in the crook of its left arm. Two huge blank eye sockets looked me up and down, taking in my uniform, but it was impossible to read any expression from the skull that peered out from under the cowl.

James Morris wasn't the only one who apparently had an appointment with Death tonight. But I knew it wasn't my time to die, and it was Halloween night. I smiled at the figure and showed it my badge.

"Agneta Dottasen, Seattle Police. I'm here on official business. Is this the Morris residence?"

I looked at Death as he looked at me. "You're early," he said, slowly raising the mask and dropping the cowl. The voice and the features that looked back at me were all too familiar, even without the motorcycle helmet I'd last seen him wearing.

I might not have believed in the supernatural, but I do think there are things about this world that we can't explain. However, the shock of seeing James Morris standing in the doorway, wearing the robes of the Grim Reaper, left me speechless for a long moment.

When I finally got my head together, I only thought of one thing to say. "And I'm sorry to say you're late, Mr. Morris."

"I just had to stay long enough to thank you, officer. You were kinder to me than I deserved."

And that was when he slowly started to fade from sight. Even the open doorway faded, leaving a still closed front door behind. My heart was a little lighter as I reached out to knock, and I let the young man's last words settle in my heart as I prepared to meet his family...

April Fool (Prequels #5)

Chapter One

April 1st 1987 - 07:12 am

ART

It had been a very long weekend, and then Monday came around and made things even worse. Strange things had been happening around the Devils Own, and there had been more Fae visitors than usual.

The build-up to April Fool's Day was always a time of great amusement to many of the Fae. It was, after all, one of the few times that they felt comfortable coming out to the mortal realm and pranking people. Not only were the Fae the originators of the April Fool prank, but they were experts in the craft. It was considered an art form by many.

So, you can imagine my trepidation as the yearly event got closer, and more Fae descended on the Devils Own than ever before. Sure, we sometimes got a couple of them, but the bar was usually quiet, and they were never any trouble. Unlike myself, they were true experts at shapeshifting and could become anything or anyone they chose. However, I was reasonably sure from their scents that most of the Fae I'd been seeing lately were not locals, and I knew most of the regulars at the bar. Along with their new faces, they had also brought their own brand of trouble.

All of which brought me to this morning, April Fool's Day itself, and the errand I was running for the Pack Alpha. Lousie Parsons had somehow got into trouble with one of the Fae, and I'd been told to 'sort things out.' I wondered if the Alpha chose me because I knew her parents.

My reflections were cut short as a sharp smell drifted through the car's open window. I couldn't pin the scent down because it seemed to change from moment to moment. At first, there appeared to be an electrical edge to the smell, but then I thought it was something burning, and finally, it seemed to settle on something woody.

I was crossing over a bridge in the middle of Seattle, just at the edge of Lake Union. There should have been no way I could pick up on the scent of the damp moss, bark, or even ferns over the stench of traffic fumes. Instead, I inhaled the odor of trees in the fall, several months away. Admittedly, there was a breeze, but the nearest woodland that could have provided this combination of scents was over a half-hour drive away.

As I tried to figure out where the smells came from and what they meant, a shadow fell over my car, blotting out the sun.

A vast gray mass of an arm had wrapped itself around the side of the bridge. The hand at the end was large enough to grab a passing car. And it was then I remembered where I was, and the date sank in all over again. I was on the Aurora Bridge. It was April Fool's Day, and someone had decided to summon the troll. I'd heard rumors that one had moved into town but had dismissed them as nothing more than that. Obviously, I'd been wrong.

My car slowed down, through no action on my part, becoming slow to respond. No matter how hard I put my foot down on the accelerator, I couldn't coax any additional speed from the vehicle. My car came to a complete halt before it could escape the shadow.

In a moment of panic, I turned the engine off and tried to restart it but got nothing more than a few half-hearted attempts at turning it over. And in that instant, I knew the car wasn't going anywhere, so I tried to get out the door.

I pulled on the handle and tried to push the door open, ripping my seatbelt off as I leaned over. But at that point, the enormous gray hand fully enveloped the car, and darkness settled over its interior.

It was probably just as well that I couldn't see anything because I heard the steel framework protesting at the unexpected pressures being applied to it. I said a quick prayer, just in case anyone was listening, before I blacked out.

***

Fremont

I close my hand upon the steel and find it feels so very real.

At first, I think to squeeze and crush, but then I concentrate, and thus

To Eldarwylde, I pull that thing to force man's wolfen blood to sing.

T'will be a marvel to behold, to see his wolf so proud and bold.

But such a change doth take a while to turn a human to something vile.

Yet I'll watch and ponder on and let wolf grow 'til man is gone.

I plan to offer it a truth and aim the wolf at failing youth.

At one whose presence I detest, I pulled her here at demon behest.

To kill by tooth, by claw, by wolf, or else I will fall 'neath master's hoof.

I watch until the man's near gone, and all that's left the wolfen one.

I tell a tale that will spark woe and end the life of a hated foe.

***

Art

The pain and disorientation of the change from human to wolf were unlike anything I'd felt in a long time. No transformation had twisted me up like this since I'd first learned to control it in my childhood.

I woke up with the change already in progress and was too far along to manage buttons and zippers. That meant I couldn't undress without ripping my clothing apart and always maintained a hardwearing wardrobe. There was only one thing to do: try to ride out the change and hope my clothes didn't prove so constrictive as to cause injuries.

As my bones and muscles moved over each other, rearranging themselves, I could feel the fabric and seams of my clothes being stretched to their limits. Usually taking mere seconds, this change took much longer than usual under ideal circumstances. As much as I tried to fight against it, nothing seemed to work, and the further the change progressed, the more restrictive the clothing would become. I'd heard tales of lupines that had become entangled in their clothes and were later found strangled by them, but this was the first time I believed it possible.

I tried to think about things that I valued about being human. I'd fought to restrain the wolf for a long time, and as I shed my first tears of frustration, I realized that it was already too late to reverse what was happening to me. Instead, I moved my concentration to try to ascertain where I was.

The landscape around me seemed mostly woodland, but I didn't recognize any species of trees. I wasn't familiar with any trees that were this shade of green, at least not without being completely moss-covered. The foliage looked out of focus as if it wasn't entirely there or made of something wispy or transparent. Without closer inspection, it could have been either or both.

The dense, low-lying fog was a lighter shade of green than the trees and seemed to cling to everything for about the first foot. Worse yet, a sickly-sweet stench seemed to drift with the fast-moving flow of the fog across the ground.

I expected the smell to get worse as I got closer to my wolf form, but that wasn't the case. Was something affecting the senses of my beast, or was there a supernatural element to the smell?

My color perception also remained unaffected. The only thing that changed was my perspective on the world. As my eyeline lowered, I dropped onto my front paws and started to look around, searching for the cause of my predicament.

It wasn't until I looked up toward the sky that I realized I'd been experiencing the environment with my animal senses the entire time I'd been here. This shouldn't have been possible without me granting the animal inside more control over me than I was happy to allow. Ever since I'd first found out what I was, it had been a constant fight to retain my humanity, and I was far from happy about my current situation.

As my transformation neared its completion, my clothes shredded and fell around me. I was grateful that even in wolf form, I was larger than average; otherwise, those seams would likely have held firm.

I was now completely naked to the elements. The fog was so low-lying I would have been shivering if not for the fur that had grown in with my transformation. Of course, that warmth would only last so long if I couldn't shed some of the moisture building up between the layers of fur. It felt like the fog was trying to crawl into my skin, and I felt an icy burn as the first droplets touched my flesh. I shivered even more and then shook myself off. This simple act seemed to loosen my fur enough to start shedding the water.

Something moved at the edge of the woods, and my beast caught the motion before I could consciously register it. My head shot around to face the massive creature, and I felt a flash of something that I usually wouldn't have tolerated from myself – fear. But if anything justified fear, this creature would be it. It was massive, malformed, and covered in moss. I'd heard tales of trolls from some of my Fae customers but had always dismissed them... Until now.

There was a familiarity about this creature that I couldn't place at first. But as it lumbered toward me and reached out its hand, it all came flooding back to me.

The massive paw was the same one that had eclipsed my drive over the Aurora Bridge and hauled my car into the air as if it had weighed nothing. Now I could see it clearly; I knew exactly what I was facing, the most enormous troll I'd ever heard tale of... Fremont!

The creature looked bulky enough to have substantial mass, but it moved with a grace and smoothness that spoke of Fae origins. Its moss-covered body would have blended in well with the surrounding woodlands if it wasn't in the middle of the clearing and reaching out to grab me.

Since I was in wolf form, and this creature was so much bigger, a huge part of me wanted to roll over, bear my throat and belly, and let it decide if I deserved to live. But a significant part of me fought to reign in that self-defeating urge. It was screaming that I needed to leave there as quickly as possible.

I spun on the spot toward the densest patch of fog. But that hand grabbed me for the second time today and plucked me into the air as if I weighed nothing.

In one instant, the creature was a blur of rapid motion, and then it stopped dead, not even appearing to breathe. In the next instant, I was somehow facing that huge singular silver eye, with no memory of having passed through the intervening space.

The move had been so fast that it should have snapped me in two, but I didn't feel any new pains beyond those associated with the forced transformation. And then I remembered that many travelers to the Eldarwylde had reported that time sometimes felt disjointed or seemed to skip entire minutes or hours.

If the troll could predict these phenomena and use them to its advantage, I would be in grave trouble.

As I realized this, the troll finally spoke for the first time since it had grabbed my car off the bridge.

"Summoned here to Eldarwylde, thou shalt find the errant child. Of your world, and not of mine, she hath caused a troubled time. A killer of many of us, our hunters she has evaded thus. Find this child and end her life, and I shall return thee to thy fife."

Between the rhyming and archaic language, it took me a few moments to figure out what it had said. But when I did, I understood why it had brought me here. Before committing myself to its quest, I wanted proof of the creature's assertions, but the beast inside wanted this more than I cared to admit.

The troll must have read my mind or guessed that I might be reluctant, and a pool of light shone onto the mist. And just like that, I was watching misty images of bodies ripped apart with such violence that I wanted to throw up. However, the beast inside me growled, recognizing a danger that might be worse than the troll. It wanted to face this new enemy head-on rather than run in fear. While I might not have agreed with the reasons, the decision was made – whether I liked it or not.

Chapter Two

April 1st 1987 - 07:25 am

Cooperfield

My eyes snapped open, and I immediately regretted even that simple motion as light bombarded my eyes. Even muted, the light brought a pounding headache that would likely haunt me for the day.

Reaching a hand up to try and cover my eyes, I encountered an unexpected wetness. Looking at my hand, I saw blood, and everything started to come back to me. I'd been driving to the office, crossing the Aurora Bridge, when something had hit me from out of nowhere. I must have blacked out from the impact because I didn't remember anything after that initial collision. And that made me even more confused as I looked around me.

The forest clearing was covered in a light greenish, foul-smelling mist that drifted randomly. It explained why my clothes were damp but not why that dampness caused my skin to itch.

After the accident, I would have expected to wake up in an ambulance, in a hospital bed, in the remains of my car, or on the banks of Lake Union. Instead, I'd woken up in the woodlands, and since there had been no forested areas along my route to work, I was concerned that I might have been abducted.

The rattle and hum of commuter traffic were gone, and the air smelled too sweet to be city air, so I had to be some distance from where the crash had occurred. That left me with the biggest concern of all. If I'd been kidnapped and then dumped out in the wilderness, what were my abductor's goals? It couldn't have been for ransom money because I had no funds to draw from or any living family members to blackmail.

I'd also never heard of a single ransom case where the abductee had been released into the wild before providing proof of life for those being blackmailed.

The aim had to be something else; I had no idea what. As I tried to figure out my next move, my hand wandered down to my hip and found the reassuring weight of my pistol and holster. Just seeing that neither had been lost was a relief. The holster would be easy enough to replace, but replacing the gun would require a ton of paperwork.

I started to circle the clearing, trying to get the lay of the land. If I had been abducted and then dragged out here, then I would have to find a vehicle. If I couldn't, I was going to have to find my way back to civilization before my captors found me.

The fog cleared for a moment, and I saw the wreckage of a car stuck up in one of the trees on the other side of the clearing. The bodywork had been destroyed in places, and curiosity pulled me to take a closer look.

A couple of thoughts went through my mind. Firstly, why was there a car halfway up a tree? There was nothing above the tree that could have supported the car's weight or from which the car could have fallen. Nor was there any damage to the upper branches, so the car hadn't fallen into the tree. Instead, the debris radiated away from the clearing as if the car had been thrown into the tree. I couldn't think of a single scenario where that would be possible.

The other thing that struck me was how much the car looked like it had been picked up by a massive hand. The way the panels and framework were bent looked like someone had grabbed a handful of clay and then squeezed.

When I reached the tree, a third thought struck. I must have had a concussion or other head trauma because the foliage on the trees closest to me seemed to be hazy. Maybe my eyes were out of focus, but I realized I was looking at a familiar vehicle.

It was the exact car I'd been driving when the accident occurred. With the fog tickling around my ankles, the whole scene took on a very dreamlike quality. No matter how hard I tried, I couldn't convince my brain that this was anything other than a dream.

Well, it wouldn't hurt to explore the dream some more, so I started to pace the perimeter of the clearing. After a few minutes, I spotted something hanging awkwardly in one of the trees. At first, I thought it might have been bait set by a hunter to catch one of the larger predators I'd heard prowled the wilds outside Seattle.

I was about to leave it hanging there, but something caught my attention, and I had to look closer. I seemed to be doing a lot of that in this dream.

I was looking at a body of some kind, though I couldn't even begin to guess what it had once been. There was no semblance to any creature I was familiar with, though I admit I'm no animal expert. There were horns, spines, and other features that I was familiar with, but their presence on an otherwise humanoid body was unusual.

Some of the wounds were reminiscent of something having been ripped from the flesh. Nubs of raw muscle hung loose, and I realized that whatever this creature had once been, something had once grown out of its back—possibly even wings.

Part of me wanted to investigate the remains further, but their stench put me off. Their very existence suggested that wherever I was in this dream, I wasn't safe, and unless I woke up, whatever had killed this creature could be coming for me next.

That thought worried me far more than I wanted to admit, but I kept my eyes open. As I looked deeper into the woods, I saw several more bodies hanging from the trees. Every single one looked as though it was tied or nailed to the tree in some way. And worse still, they looked like fresh kills.

I was instantly on edge and pinched myself, trying to wake myself from the dream. Even though the trick had worked in the past, it failed me on this occasion, and I started to doubt I was dreaming.

Somewhere in the distance, a wolf howled, and there was an undertone of pain in that voice as if the poor thing were crying out for help. It made me wonder if whatever had killed the creatures around me was now hunting that wolf, and I was not inclined to find out.

I started to back away from the howling, slowly edging across the clearing, and then, as the howling stopped, I heard a new sound.

Something huge crashed through the trees some distance away, and I suspected that whatever it was had something to do with the carnage in the tree line.

I hoped the creature was a large bear, but I doubted it would be so simple because of the deformities in the bodies I'd seen so far. After all, dreams rarely played fair, and this one had already become a nightmare I wanted to wake from.

I tried to pinch myself again, but nothing changed except my level of anxiety.

***

Fremont

By sacred mirrors scrying powers, I sit and watch my toys for hours.

To see if they will play by rules, or if instead, will act the fools.

Oh, foe by bodies grave perturbed, the wolf will leave your world disturbed.

One little trick I think shall find; a world of enemies combined.

A simple push shall stir the leaves and cause the metal box to heave

And watch my foe scamper clear of forest clearing full of fear.

To race away among the trees, let us check if wolf-man sees.

Ah yes, explosion turns his head but fills his soul with fear and dread.

The two shall surely meet up soon, and I will earn my master's boon.

And wolfman will devour our foe, 'cos that is how I will it so.

***

Cooperfield

A stiff wind blew through the clearing, and the trees started to shake in response. As the winds strengthened, I realized there was an excellent chance the car could be thrown back out of the tree. Just as I was thinking about it, I heard several branches snap, and the vehicle dropped a few inches and then slipped even further.

I ran from the clearing as my car dropped from the tree and did what should have been impossible – it exploded. I threw myself to the ground and curled into a ball, trying to present as small a target as possible. Shards of hot metal flew out of the fireball, and I felt one tear through the sleeve of my suit.

When the violence of the moment passed, I picked myself up to check for injuries. When I found none, I breathed a sigh of relief and started to circle the clearing again. I was looking for a path, even an animal trail, which would be sufficient to lead me away from the spreading fire.

Smoke blew in my direction as if following me, no matter where I went. Even though I had to rush my search, I started to get the feeling that I was being watched. It wasn't a feeling I liked, and the hairs on my neck bristled at the sensation.

I couldn't pinpoint what gave me the feeling, but I was far enough away from the bodies in the trees that I couldn't see them. Since bodies didn't come back to life, there was something else out there, and whatever it was had likely killed them.

As I was thinking about this, I realized that the crashing noises had stopped when the winds had picked up. Whatever was out in the woods had caught new prey or decided to rest. Considering everything

I'd seen, I prayed it had chosen the latter option because I didn't wish that kind of fate on any creature.

I tried to resist the need to locate whatever was watching me, but the more I tried, the more unsettled I became. I forced myself to stop thinking about it before I started spinning in circles, trying to find the source of the impression.

Something rustled in the undergrowth, but I couldn't see anything clearly because of the fog. All I had to go on was the movement of an indistinct shadow. Whatever it was had been large enough to draw my attention but too small to have been the cause of the crashing noises I had heard earlier.

At first, I didn't feel too worried since I could have just been watching the motion of leaves being blown around in the slight breeze. But when the rustling came again, I realized something was circling the edge of the clearing. I reached down to my hip, unclipped the catch on my holster, and felt the familiar texture of the pistol grip settle into my palm.

I didn't draw immediately because I've never believed in pulling a weapon unless you were sure you had exhausted all other options. Once you pull a gun, matters escalate fast, and you must be ready to pull that trigger without hesitation, or it could cost you your life.

So far in the line of duty, I'd pulled my gun seven times and fired it on six of those occasions. Not once had it been necessary to kill my target. But if whatever was out there came at me and was responsible for the bodies in the woods, then I had no doubt that today it'd be kill or be killed.

The pistol grip in my hand gave me something solid to focus on. I started believing I could escape this dream with my sanity intact. It was just a case of holding on until...

And there it was again, that rustling...

I spun toward the sound, and the shape that emerged from the tree line was unmistakable.

A colossal wolf strode forward, its bulk suggesting that it was well-fed and capable of hunting well enough to support its substantial bulk. Its eyes were focused on me as a growl started in the back of its throat, and it approached slowly.

There was no caution in its posture as it started to gather speed. My gun was out of its holster, lined up, and the bullet in the air before I even realized I had reacted.

Chapter Three

April 1ˢᵗ 1987 - 10:23 Am

Art

The animal in me reacted to the gun even before I heard the sound. My beast shifted its focus to the woman as I kept moving toward her. At the same time, something hot passed through the fur along the top of my head.

A thwack behind me suggested that the object had hit one of the trees. I wanted to turn and run, but instinct insisted that the woman was a threat, and my life was in immediate danger. Considering how close that shot had come to taking the top of my head off, I couldn't help but agree.

I hated letting the beast take control, but if I didn't, there was a good chance I'd freeze when the moment came to strike. The hunter wanted blood; I couldn't force it back into submission this time.

Everything except the woman and the weapon faded into a blur as the beast focused on moving forward until the exact moment to attack. I want to say that it was cold and calculating, but fear and anger were boiling beneath my instincts.

It was like watching myself from the outside as the beast took complete control and increased its pace with every step.

The woman's eyes widened, and her breath quickened as she saw the animal's intent. I could see her trying to relax enough to steady herself for a second shot. But the beast acted, and my back paws pushed hard against the firm ground, launching me into the air.

My jaws opened wide, and the creature inside focused on striking its target. Its paws came up to absorb some of the impact, and I felt my head snap around as I flew toward the woman.

There was a second bang, and my proximity to the sound almost deafened me.

***

Cooperfield

I regretted not having fired a moment sooner, as the shot missed, and tens of pounds of wolf flew toward me.

Its jaws clamped down on my wrist, and I screamed in pain as its weight barreled into my torso, carrying me down to the ground with sheer momentum. The force of the blow almost tore the teeth from my arm, and I was grateful that they clamped down harder rather than ripping a massive chunk of flesh away. And then the pain registered, and I wasn't so sure about my gratitude.

I hit the ground, and a jolt ran through my arm. My hand spasmed, and I lost my grip on the gun. It fell out of my hand as I rolled hard. I thrashed with my free arm and bucked repeatedly, trying to dislodge the weight of the massive canine.

The beast's greater mass and hunting experience gave it a massive advantage. Its paws dug into my belly as the head whipped around. With that same motion, my arm was pulled up before me, and I didn't even try to resist. If I had any chance of winning this fight, I couldn't afford to lose the use of a hand.

As its head turned to face me, I saw something unexpected. Those eyes had an intelligence that surpassed anything I'd seen in any dog. But then I tried to remind myself that this was no ordinary dog but a born hunter.

I was more spooked than I had any right to be, and I started flailing around with my free hand as I watched my blood drip from this creature's jaws.

Twisting, turning, and bucking with all my strength did nothing against the weight, and I felt myself starting to panic.

***

Art

Something wasn't right about this setup. The woman had gone down too quickly, and a look in her eyes suggested she was terrified.

She'd remained calm enough to try and take two potshots at me, but her aim hadn't been steady, and the shots missed even at point blank. Her hands had been shaking. The devastation that the troll had shown me was the work of a stone-cold killer. That kind of person wouldn't miss at such close range, even with a beast like me barreling down on them. It should have been two quick shots to the head and maybe another to the heart.

And now, in her desperation and fear, she was trying to throw me aside as if I were more her weight and size. I had a considerable advantage in weight and experience, but fear gave her a surprising amount of strength.

That was when I made a decision that could end up being my downfall. The wolf wouldn't like what I had in mind now that it had tasted blood. Nevertheless, I was going to try trusting the women. She wasn't the one who'd dragged me here and wanted to turn me into a furry assassin. She'd shot at me in self-defense, which likely made her as much of a victim in all of this as I was.

Taking a deep breath, I jumped off her chest, eliciting a large whooshing sound as my paws drove the air from her lungs. Thankfully, the move left her incapacitated just long enough for me to put some distance between us.

I was a little concerned about the wounds I'd caused, but there was nothing I could do about them in my current form. It was taking everything I had not to turn completely wild at the scent of blood.

A thought struck me. If this woman wasn't the killer the troll had told me she was, then he had lied to me. And if that was the case, then there was a good chance of other illusions in this setup. Something had forced me to shift to wolf form on arrival in the Eldarwylde, but what if that had also been part of the troll's lies?

I tried to shift back to human form, and though the forced shift to wolf had been bad, this was worse. I could feel the wolf fighting to keep control. It had only ever done this in the presence of extreme danger, and I would have listened to it now, but I didn't dare. If something was out there more dangerous than me or this woman, I had to find a way to communicate the need for cooperation. I couldn't do that in the form I was currently trapped in.

I struggled to force my animal back into the mental and emotional cage that I usually kept it locked in. At every twist and turn of the fight, I could feel claws running through my thoughts and a wave of anger and frustration that demanded release. It was one of the most brutal fights of my life.

The woman gasped, suggesting the internal turmoil manifested in the outer struggle to change forms. The pain was unbearable, but I dug deep into the core of who I was and kept fighting. Letting the pain overwhelm me would likely lead me to pass out and leave the wolf in complete control.

I had been born with this supposed gift, and at best, I indulged the beast within to maintain what little sanity I could hang onto. It constantly demanded release, and maybe that had something to do with the difficulties I had returning to human form. But in the end, sheer stubbornness won out, and I finally managed to stagger onto two feet.

But the victory came at a cost, and as I adjusted to standing upright, the world tilted suddenly, and I passed out.

I couldn't have been out long because the sun had barely moved. It shone from behind the woman, and I was almost blind. However, that didn't stop me from making out enough of her silhouette to tell she had the gun pointed right at my head.

"You won't need that," I said softly, trying not to make any moves that might seem hasty or threatening.

"And why the hell do you think I should trust you? Whatever you are... Are you the one behind all this?" She swung her head around the clearing, and the gun didn't waver. She believed she was in control of the situation, which made her comfortable and boosted her confidence. Her words made me feel this was her first time dealing with the supernatural. She was doing better than most.

"You can't trust me. Your only experience of me is of me trying to rip your hand off rather than letting you shoot me in the face." I knew this was likely a bad gambit, but I wouldn't lie to her. I couldn't tell why, but I didn't feel the need or the inclination. Maybe she had innate magic, like the psychics, or perhaps I sensed something about her that made me want her trust. But I'd certainly given her no reason to trust me.

***

Cooperfield

I left the creature pinned down, with my gun pointed at its head, until I was sure it wasn't going to do anything stupid. I'd already had too many surprises today and wasn't about to be caught out by another one.

"So... Who, and what the hell are you?" I demanded, keeping my aim as steady as I could. It had been almost five minutes since this thing had passed out, and now that it was conscious, I wanted answers. Among the first of them was why it had been writhing around and howling in pain, cursing and swearing at something or someone I couldn't see.

It remained quiet for a moment longer than I liked, and I waved the gun while locking eyes with the creature. I would get some answers or start shooting, but I wasn't too particular about which.

"My name is Art. You don't need to know the rest, for the moment. As for what I am. I'm not sure you're ready for that answer." I shouldn't have locked eyes with him. His eyes showed warmth and deep-seated pain, and I melted into that gaze.

A shake of my head was all it took to break the look and bring me back to my senses. I couldn't afford to start feeling sorry for this beast if I wanted to escape these woods. I didn't trust this Art, but with his help, I might make it out of these woods before whatever had committed the atrocious killings found me.

"If you put the gun away, I'll help figure out a way to get us back to our world. Neither one of us would survive here for long without the other. There are things here that neither of us wants to try fighting. Please. Just trust me until we get back to civilization."

I wasn't sure I could rule him out as the cause of the carnage, but if he wasn't responsible for that, his words made a lot of sense... except for the part about getting back to 'our world.'

I made the mistake of looking down at him again, and my tired, trembling arms turned traitor. I couldn't tell you if muscle fatigue or something in his eyes swayed me, but the gun suddenly felt so heavy.

As I holstered the gun, I heard a bellow rage off in the distance. In the same instant, a fierce wind whipped up out of nowhere, causing the fog to billow around us. The fog became so thick that it obscured the woodlands, and I couldn't see as far down as my feet.

When the air cleared, I could smell the familiar scent of the city again and felt a cool sea breeze blowing over me. I stood in the shade of a bridge, and everything looked normal again. But hours had passed, and the streetlights were coming on. Even with the extra light, I still worried about that rage-filled creature coming after us.

"Oh, don't worry about the troll. The way between the worlds has probably closed behind us. From what little I know of these things, the gateways rarely last past nightfall."

I had a feeling that Art knew what he was saying, and now that we were back in familiar surroundings, it seemed like he was becoming more human by the second. I still had no reason to trust him, but I reached down to help him. Despite our size differences, he accepted the help with good grace, especially considering I'd been holding him at gunpoint a couple of minutes ago.

The moon crept out from behind a cloud as he looked at me. My heart melted, and I blushed as I realized some things. Firstly, he must have said something because he looked at me slightly concerned as he repeated himself.

"You've had a shocking encounter, I know. But if you still want some answers, I'll explain what little I can. I warn you, though, you might think I'm crazy before I'm done."

If he'd caught me staring, he didn't indicate it, but I felt like a little schoolgirl with her first crush, and it felt good. Somehow, I knew something good would come from knowing Art, but I had no idea how he'd shape the next few years of my life.

But now we were back in familiar territory, and I couldn't ignore the second thing I'd noticed. And I felt the heat rising to my cheeks for the second time in an amazingly short period. Even more interestingly, I felt that Art hadn't noticed what I had.

My hand returned to my pistol because I wasn't sure how he'd take my next words.

"Um... Art? You'd better get some clothes on before someone asks me to arrest you for indecent exposure."

Chapter Four

April 1st 1987 – 10:57 am

Fremont

Their trust my spell hath undone. My plan today was all for none.

My wolfen hunter failed his task, to bring the human down at last.

His beast defied, his role denied. It's like he never even tried

To keep the bargain we had struck. The woman had a run of luck.

That will bring me naught but grief, for together I see them sleep.

And from that union comes a child, who's powers will be far and wild

My master's plans shall come undone, who will he blame? There's only one.

So, I now sit and plan anew, and for a year I'll stop and stew

Await my time to destroy the one, who's birth and time are yet to come.

For without her strength and subtle power, our greatest foe will lose her hour

To call on beasts in forests hid, to wait and fight like they once did

To overthrow my master's deeds, and subtly to plant the seeds

That his power base will destroy, and leave me stranded like a boy

Without hope, nor hope to see, the world that's terrified of me

And in my prison I'll remain, to see daylight never once again.

The Challenge (Prequels #6)

Chapter One

ART

I had a lot on my mind as I watched my pack members gather for the first time in weeks. Several out-of-town vampires had come to Seattle looking to challenge the status quo, which was causing problems for the master vampire and my own people. There had been an uneasy peace between the vampires and the shapeshifters, forged when I discovered a blood relationship with the master vampire and used that to build bonds between us.

But those bonds had become strained when the new-bloods arrived and started hunting my pack members. As their alpha, I was responsible for keeping them safe, so I contacted the master vampire for guidance on how he wanted to address the matter. I didn't want to interfere in any plan he had to take care of the new-bloods, but I wasn't going to let these attacks continue.

His assurances that he would take care of the problem were far from reassuring, especially after I discovered that several of his own people were taking part in the most recent hunts. So, I called the pack to update everyone on what was happening and how I wanted it handled. I didn't trust technology when it came to matters as important as keeping my people informed because it was so impersonal. I wanted everyone to see my face and how seriously I took matters. But more importantly, I wanted them all to hear the news at the same time to prevent any further rumors.

The moon hung behind the trees, casting moving patterns of light and shadow in the warm breeze. I could tell it had rained recently because of how the earth beneath my feet smelled and the freshness of the wet pines. Even in human form, those scents were strong, but in wolf form, I'd have picked up even more.

I looked around the group in the clearing and began checking names and faces off my mental list. A few were missing for personal reasons, and a couple were in the hospital due to injuries from vampire attacks. Everyone else was there, except for a couple of very notable exceptions.

I was disappointed because I had specifically wanted them here. Their support was needed for my plan to protect as many pack members as possible to work. The roles I intended for them to take on were crucial to ensuring everything went smoothly.

There were a few more minutes before I'd scheduled the meeting to start, so I ran through my security precautions in case the vampires took advantage of our gathering.

We had gathered in pack-owned territory, so everyone knew where the escape routes were. Every approach was guarded by at least two pack members with fighting experience. They would remain within earshot of the clearing to hear what was happening. But if a threat were spotted, one of the guards would engage any intruders, while the other would communicate the scale and nature of the threat so I could devise an appropriate response. We'd used this tactic in the past and it had proved effective.

Over thirty pack members were present, so we could probably handle most threats. But that didn't warrant taking any chances.

I gave the last stragglers a few minutes to arrive and then called for silence. The chatter stopped instantly, but I could hear the unasked questions hanging in the air. Raising my voice so all could hear, I dove straight into why we were gathered.

"It has been a while since we gathered as a pack like this, and I wish we were meeting under different circumstances." I heard muttering from the back of the gathering but didn't let it interrupt me. "We're here to discuss the rumors that have been flying around and address them."

Questions were shouted into the silence as I paused for breath, and I had to bring everyone back to order. "I WILL have order! We're lupines, not a pack of terrified strays!" I let that sink in before continuing. "First... The vampires do not want a war, so WE will NOT start one. Second... These attacks are the work of a handful of new-bloods and a couple of sympathizers. The master vampire does NOT sanction them and has asked that we allow him to deal with the problem. Third... I have a plan to make sure this ends peacefully."

I allowed everyone to absorb this information because it was important that no one went off half-cocked. I'd seen what a war between lupines and vampires could result in, and I was not going to let that happen to my people.

"Thus far, we've lost no members of the pack, and I don't intend to let that happen. So, we will do what we've always done in times of trouble. We'll check in with each other regularly, report any missed check-ins, defend ourselves as needed, and look out for each other. I'm looking for two volunteers to help keep us coordinated."

I saw three hands go up and picked the two lupines I knew best. I'd hoped not to have to ask for volunteers, but the two I wanted to step up had failed to show. To say I was disappointed in them was an understatement.

"I know not all of you are comfortable fighting, but if you have to defend yourself, do whatever it takes to disengage from the fight and call in help. Those of you who are ready to fight... come see me after the meeting, and we'll..."

A disturbance at one of the guard posts stopped me as I tried to establish what was happening. The guards hadn't called for assistance, but something felt wrong. I reached out to the part of me that I tried to keep at bay and summoned a portion of my beast. Just enough to pick up the scents of those present and the familiar odor of one of the two missing pack members.

I could see her trying to push through the lupines who stood in her way, and I called for them to let her through.

Chapter Two

SARAH

I pushed through the last two lupines who had been in my way, even as they parted at the Alpha's command. And there he stood, in the center of a ring of lupines, two or three deep in places, turning his back on me as if to address the pack again. I was sick of being dismissed so easily, of being treated like a child and, at the same time, part of the pack and an outsider.

Well, he was about to get the biggest surprise of his life.

I stepped forward into the ring of lupines and raised my voice so that even the guards would hear me clearly.

"Alpha, I challenge you by the right of blood. By the needs of the pack. And by the will of the ancient ones. Your people need a new leader!" I didn't need to use the old form to make the challenge, but doing so made it irreversible. Either he accepted the call to defend his place at the head of the pack or would have to step aside and relinquish his people to my leadership. If he wasn't ready to take the fight to the vampires, then he didn't deserve to lead.

The look of surprise on his face and the apparent shock running through the gathering told me that the timing of my challenge was having the effect I wanted. I heard people wondering what was happening, how I thought I had the right to challenge, and why now...

I watched as the Alpha pulled himself together and tried to figure out how to respond. I was of age, and my challenge was legal. He just didn't realize it, and his next words proved how little he knew of me.

"You might be old enough to challenge me. But you are not a lupine, and your challenge is invalid. We will talk more about this later. Here and now is NOT the time."

He moved to turn his back on me again, and I stepped into the center of the gathering and put my hand on his arm.

"You're right. I am old enough. But you're also wrong. It turns out I am just a late bloomer…" Most lupines went through their first change in early childhood. I'd gone through my first only weeks ago, shortly after my seventeenth birthday. And I'd learned a lot in that time.

I stepped back and unzipped the loose dress I'd picked for this occasion. It fell to the grass, leaving me fully exposed to everyone's eyes and a little self-conscious. But I'd come here for a purpose and wouldn't let anything stop me.

"Your people need someone to fight for them, Alpha. I may be your daughter, but you will face my challenge or step aside. Prove you're still worthy to lead, and I will withdraw. Fail, and I will do what must be done for the good of the pack."

I shifted to my wolf form, dropping onto all fours, revealing for the first time that I was truly one of the pack and that my challenge was incontestable. The warm breeze played through my fur as I adjusted to wolf form.

He started stripping, preparing to make his own shift, and I heard him mutter a plea just before he changed.

"Don't make me do this. PLEASE!" And those were the last words from his mouth before his change was completed, and our two wolf forms faced off, with the pack as witness.

The wolf before me was larger and more experienced, but I had the advantage of being smaller and faster, at least in human form. I'd learned this growing up when he'd played with me as a child. Those occasions had been all too few since he and my mother had divorced, and she had won custody. So, I was counting on surprise to give me the edge.

I darted forward in the instant before his change was complete, taking the initiative and using the moments of sensory adjustment after a change to my advantage. I swiped at his flank and bit at his leg, intending to wound him and take away part of his size advantage. But he turned and shouldered me aside, turning faster than I had thought possible. He was trying not to hurt me, but I had no such qualms.

I kept him circling as I stayed just out of range of his jaws. I darted in and out every time he exposed a flank. But he was too experienced to let me get in close enough to do any damage, so I kept him moving, hoping to wear him down.

Unfortunately, he seemed to have more stamina than I'd given him credit for. This was going to be a long-drawn-out fight if one of us didn't do something unexpected.

I rushed him from the side, and my jaws caught his lower jaw. I clamped down, feeling my teeth get purchase, and raised my paws to try and strike his throat. But he just raised his head, and I hung on for dear life as he thrashed his head around, trying to throw me off.

Chapter Three

RICHARD

I was late as I rushed up the trail toward the meeting spot. There was some kind of commotion from the meeting, and the guards seemed distracted as I approached. It was all too easy to slip past them, and I knew I would have to speak with Art about his supposed security.

Growls came from up ahead, and I pushed through the crowd of lupines just in time to see a young wolf attack Art. I couldn't tell who was stupid enough to attack the hulking Alpha, but if what I'd heard was true, now was not the time to fight among ourselves. I knew how strong and powerful Art was; he was intimidating in either form. He'd made me back down more than a few times in the time since he'd known me.

I pushed to the front of the crowd, thinking that someone would have to end this fight, but the young wolf's inexperience suddenly showed.

Art feigned an opening for her to attack, and she did something neither I nor Art had expected. She rushed him and somehow got her jaws clamped around his. And Art took full advantage of her mistake. He shook his head back and forth and threw her bodily across the clearing. Her small form crashed against a tree, and I heard something snap from the force of the impact.

Whoever this lupine woman was, she was either brave or stupid because I saw her trying to rise from where she'd fallen.

The alpha closed in on her slowly, and something in his movements spoke of deliberate anger. It was the same kind of anger I saw every time I'd stood up to him, and I knew that this young wolf was about to pay the price of trying to face off against the Alpha. He was going to force her to back off, or... No... he wouldn't kill her. That wasn't in his nature.

But if she'd challenged his leadership, he had to make an example of her.

As I watched everything unfold in slow motion, her eyes turned to me, and I saw something familiar in them. I knew who she was and that either she or the Alpha was about to make a costly mistake.

She rose unsteadily, setting her paws, ready to charge her opponent, and I made a decision I would probably regret.

I was already shifting as my clothes hit the ground, and I charged into the fray, ready to bring this fight to an end. I honestly didn't think about it. I just acted, racing to get between the two combatants and force them to step back and think.

The younger wolf was shaky on her feet, but I'd seen her stubborn streak too many times to think she'd back down. In the past, it had got her scolded, grounded, and even spanked... But here, now, it was likely to get her killed.

The Alpha and I rarely saw eye to eye, but I had to keep him from what I suspected he was about to do...

And I reached her just before he did. I shoved her back down onto the ground, and the jaws that should have closed mere inches from her snout tore into my throat.

Chapter Four

ART

I tasted blood as my jaws closed around fur, and my beast whipped my head around, tearing a chunk of flesh from the wolf that had come from nowhere.

As he fell, I finally came to my senses, the scent in my nostrils all too familiar.

Looking down at the fallen form before me made me want to howl. A chunk missing from his throat left him bleeding out, dying in a way so like his mother's death that I felt I'd failed her all over again. On the day I'd found him tired, alone, shocked by her death, and angry at the world, I'd promised to keep him safe, and now I'd killed him...

As I watched, my young challenger collapsed against the dying wolf, her strength and anger finally giving out, leaving me the victor. Yet that victory felt hollow as I watched her breathing falter, her left side crushed from hitting the tree.

Listening to her wheezing breaths, I knew there was internal damage, and I was going to lose another pack member... No, I was going to lose another child... My daughter would join my son in death. Both lost in a senseless challenge, and I'd never told him of our true connection or the love I'd had for his mother...

***

I woke sweating with the taste of blood still in my mouth and raised my hand to the pain in my lip. It came away soaked in blood, and I could smell even more on the pillow. Somehow, I'd bitten my lip in my sleep, but I didn't care.

The memory of the dream felt so real that I wondered if it was prophecy or the stress of several long days of negotiations with various factions in the city.

Either way, I knew it would haunt me, even as I reached for my phone to call the two people I cared for most in the world. I might never be brave enough to tell Richard the truth, but for now, I had to hear his voice. And then, I would call Sarah's mother and make sure my daughter was okay. I felt Sarah and I would have things to discuss, and I wanted her mother's permission first. I'd never considered whether Sarah might feel excluded from the pack, but that would be a good place to start.

Don't miss out!

Visit the website below and you can sign up to receive emails whenever Timothy Bateson publishes a new book. There's no charge and no obligation.

https://books2read.com/r/B-A-KTBLB-CIBID

BOOKS 2 READ

Connecting independent readers to independent writers.

Also by Timothy Bateson

Shadows Over Seattle
Shadows Over Seattle: Prequels 1-6

Shadows Over Seattle: Prequels
Under A Hunter's Moon (Shadows Over Seattle: Prequels One)
The Lupine's Call (Shadows Over Seattle: Prequels Two)
Wolves In The Desert (Shadows Over Seattle: Prequels Three)

Standalone
Evaline Transcendent

Watch for more at https://timothybatesonauthor.com.

About the Author

I'm a city boy at heart, growing up in the London (England) area. In 2005, I moved to rural Alaska for love, and I'm still here, writing gritty urban fantasy. What else can I say about me?

How about I love falconry, have been licked by a wolf, had a lion cub fall asleep on my lap, had close encounters with moose, and still love the big city?

Or should I tell you about the gritty urban fantasy stories that I've written? How I love diving into the minds and emotions of the characters I create? Why I let their thoughts and feelings bleed through me onto the page while trying to tell the best stories I can? Because I write the stories I want to read, I fill the page with the fantastic while keeping everything grounded in the realities I create.

I somehow manage to do all this while working a full-time job, exploring the world of AI art, and creating products for book lovers.

If you want to know more or keep up to date with my projects, please don't hesitate to contact me. I'd love to hear from you. You can also join my mailing list to receive updates directly.

Substack Newsletter Signup:

https://timothybatesonauthor.substack.com/subscribe

Read more at https://timothybatesonauthor.com.